THE HEROES OF OLYMPUS

THE
DEMIGOD
DIARIES

RICK RIORDAN

DISNEY • HYPERION BOOKS
NEW YORK

Printed in the United States of America

First Edition

1 3 5 7 9 10 8 6 4 2

G475-5664-5-12152

Library of Congress Cataloging-in-Publication Data
Riordan, Rick.
The heroes of Olympus: the demigod diaries/by Rick Riordan.—1st ed.
p. cm.—(The heroes of Olympus)
Summary: Four short stories plus original art, interviews, puzzles, and games, reveal
new insights into the world of Percy Jackson and the other heroes of Olympus.
ISBN 978-1-4231-6300-8 (hardcover)
1. Mythology, Roman—Juvenile fiction. 2. Mythology, Greek—Juvenile fiction.
[1. Mythology, Roman—Fiction. 2. Mythology, Greek—Fiction. 3. Monsters—
Fiction. 4. Diaries—Fiction.] I. Title. II. Title: Demigod diaries.
PZ7.R4829Her 2012
[Fic]—dc23   2011035609

Designed by Joann Hill

Visit www.disneyhyperionbooks.com

To the Winston School of San Antonio,
a safe place for demigods

TABLE OF CONTENTS

DEAR YOUNG DEMIGOD,

Your destiny awaits. Now that you have discovered your true parentage, you must prepare yourself for a difficult future—fighting monsters, adventuring across the world, and dealing with temperamental Greek and Roman gods. I don't envy you.

I hope this volume will help you on your journeys. I had to think long and hard before publishing these stories, as they were given to me in the strictest confidence. However, your survival comes first, and this book will give you an inside look at the world of demigods—information that may help keep you alive.

We'll begin with "The Diary of Luke Castellan." Over the years, many readers and campers at Camp Half-Blood have asked me to tell the story of Luke's early days, adventuring with Thalia and Annabeth before they arrived at camp. I have been reluctant to do this, as neither Annabeth nor Thalia likes to talk about those times. The only information I have is recorded in Luke's own handwriting, in his original diary given to me by Chiron. I think it's time, though, to share a little of Luke's story. It may help us understand what went wrong for such a promising young demigod. In this excerpt you will find out how Thalia and Luke arrived in Richmond, Virginia, chasing a magic goat, how they were almost destroyed in a house of horrors, and how they met a young girl named Annabeth.

I have also included a map of Halcyon Green's house in

Richmond. Despite the damage described in the story, the house has been rebuilt, which is very troubling. If you go there, be careful. It may still contain treasures. But it most assuredly contains monsters and traps as well.

Our second story will definitely get me in trouble with Hermes. "Percy Jackson and the Staff of Hermes" describes an embarrassing incident for the god of travelers, which he hoped to solve quietly with the help of Percy and Annabeth. Chronologically, the story happens between *The Last Olympian* and *The Lost Hero*, in the days when Percy and Annabeth had just started dating, before Percy disappeared. It's a good example of how a demigod's daily routine can be interrupted at a moment's notice by a crisis on Mount Olympus. Even if you're just going to Central Park for a picnic, always bring your sword! Hermes has threatened me with slow mail, lousy Internet service, and a horrible stock market if I publish this story. I hope he is just bluffing.

Following that story, I've provided an interview with George and Martha, Hermes's snakes, as well as portraits of important demigods you may meet during your quests. This includes the first-ever image of Thalia Grace. She really doesn't like to have her portrait drawn, but we managed to convince her just this once.

Next, "Leo Valdez and the Quest for Buford" will take you behind the scenes at Bunker 9 as Leo tries to construct his ultimate flying ship, the *Argo II* (a.k.a. "the spanking hot war machine").

You will learn that monster encounters can happen even within the boundaries of Camp Half-Blood, and in this instance, Leo gets himself into some potentially catastrophic trouble involving psychotic party girls, walking tables, and explosive materials. Even with the help of Piper and Jason, it's not clear he'll be able to survive what happens.

I'm also including a diagram of Bunker 9, though you should be aware this is only a rough sketch! No one, not even Leo, has discovered all the secret passages, tunnels, and hidden rooms of the bunker. We can only guess how big and complicated the place truly is.

Finally, the most dangerous story of all: "Son of Magic." The subject matter is so sensitive I could not write it myself. There was no way I could get close enough to the young demigod Alabaster to interview him. He would've known me as an agent of Camp Half-Blood and likely destroyed me on the spot. My son, Haley, however, was able to gain access to his secrets. Haley, who is now sixteen, the same age as Percy Jackson, wrote "Son of Magic" especially for this book, and I have to say he's managed to answer some questions that were mysteries even to me. Who controls the Mist, and how? Why are monsters able to sense demigods? What happened to the demigods who fought in Kronos's army during the invasion of Manhattan? All these questions are addressed in "Son of Magic." You will find it sheds light on an entirely new and extremely perilous part of Percy Jackson's world.

I hope *The Demigod Diaries* will help prepare you for your own adventures. As Annabeth will tell you, knowledge is a weapon. I wish you luck, young reader. Keep your armor and weapons at hand. Stay vigilant. And remember, you are not alone!

Sincerely,

Rick Riordan
Senior Scribe
Camp Half-Blood
Long Island, New York

THE DIARY

OF

LUKE CASTELLAN

MY NAME IS LUKE.

Honestly, I don't know if I'll be able to keep up with this diary. My life is pretty crazy. But I promised the old man I would try. After what happened today . . . well, I owe him.

My hands are shaking as I sit here on guard duty. I can't get the horrible images out of my head. I've got a few hours until the girls wake up. Maybe if I write down the story, I'll be able to put it behind me.

I should probably start with the magic goat.

———

For three days, Thalia and I had been following the goat across Virginia. I wasn't sure why. To me, the goat didn't look like anything special, but Thalia was more agitated than I'd ever seen her before. She was convinced the goat was some sort of sign from her dad, Zeus.

Yeah, her dad is a Greek god. So is mine. We're demigods. If you think that sounds cool, think again. Demigods are monster magnets. All those ancient Greek nasties like Furies and harpies and gorgons still exist, and they can sense heroes like us from miles away. Because of that, Thalia and I spend all our time running for our lives. Our superpowerful parents don't even talk to us, much less help us. Why? If I tried to explain that, I'd fill up this whole diary, so I'm going to move on.

Anyway, this goat would pop up at random times, always in the distance. Whenever we tried to catch up to it, the goat would vanish and appear farther away, as if it was leading us somewhere.

Me, I would've left it alone. Thalia wouldn't explain why she thought it was important, but she and I had been adventuring together long enough that I'd learned to trust her judgment. So we followed the goat.

Early in the morning, we made it into Richmond. We trudged across a narrow bridge over a lazy green river, past wooded parks and Civil War cemeteries. As we got closer to the center of town, we navigated through sleepy neighborhoods of red brick town houses wedged close together, with white-columned porches and tiny gardens.

I imagined all the normal families living in those cozy houses. I wondered what it would be like to have a home, to know where my next meal was coming from, and not have to worry about getting eaten by monsters every day. I'd run away when I was only nine—five long years ago. I barely remembered what it was like to sleep in a real bed.

After walking another mile, my feet felt like they were melting inside my shoes. I hoped we could find a place to rest, maybe get some food. Instead, we found the goat.

The street we were following opened up into a big circular park. Stately red brick mansions faced the roundabout. In the middle of the circle, atop a twenty-foot white marble pedestal, was a bronze dude sitting on horseback. Grazing at the base of the monument was the goat.

"Hide!" Thalia pulled me behind a row of rosebushes.

"It's just a goat," I said for the millionth time. "Why—?"

"It's special," Thalia insisted. "One of my dad's sacred animals. Her name is Amaltheia."

She'd never mentioned the goat's name before. I wondered why she sounded so nervous.

Thalia isn't scared of much. She's only twelve, two years younger than I am, but if you saw her walking down the street you'd clear a path. She wears black leather boots, black jeans, and a tattered leather jacket studded with punk rock buttons. Her hair is dark and choppy like a feral animal's. Her intense blue eyes bore into you as if she's considering the best way to beat you to a pulp.

Anything that scared her, I had to take seriously.

"So you've seen this goat before?" I asked.

She nodded reluctantly. "In Los Angeles, the night I ran away. Amaltheia led me out of the city. And later, that night you and I met . . . she led me to *you*."

I stared at Thalia. As far as I knew, our meeting had been an accident. We literally ran into each other in a dragon's cave outside Charleston and teamed up to stay alive. Thalia had never mentioned a goat.

As far as her old life in Los Angeles, Thalia didn't like to talk about it. I respected her too much to pry. I knew her mom had fallen in love with Zeus. Eventually Zeus dumped her, as gods tend to do. Her mom went off the deep end, drinking and doing crazy things—I didn't know the details—until finally Thalia decided to run. In other words, her past was a lot like mine.

She took a shaky breath. "Luke, when Amaltheia appears, something important is about to happen . . . something *dangerous*. She's like a warning from Zeus, or a guide."

"To what?"

"I don't know . . . but look." Thalia pointed across the street. "She's not disappearing this time. We must be close to wherever she's leading us."

Thalia was right. The goat was just standing there, less than a hundred yards away, contentedly nibbling grass at the base of the monument.

I was no expert on barnyard animals, but Amaltheia *did* look strange now that we were closer. She had curlicue horns like a ram, but the swollen udders of a girl goat. And her shaggy gray fur . . . was it glowing? Wisps of light seemed to cling to her like a cloud of neon, making her look blurry and ghostly.

A couple of cars looped around the traffic circle, but nobody seemed to notice the radioactive goat. That didn't surprise me. There's some sort of magical camouflage that keeps mortals from seeing the true appearance of monsters and gods. Thalia and I weren't sure what this force was called or how it worked, but it was pretty powerful. Mortals might see the goat as just a stray dog, or they might not see it at all.

Thalia grabbed my wrist. "Come on. Let's try to talk to it."

"First we hide from the goat," I said. "Now you want to talk to the goat?"

Thalia dragged me out of the rosebushes and pulled me across the street. I didn't protest. When Thalia gets an idea in her head, you just have to go with. She always gets her way.

Besides, I couldn't let her go without me. Thalia has saved my life a dozen times. She's my only friend. Before we met, I'd traveled for years on my own, lonely and miserable. Once in a while I'd befriend a mortal, but whenever I told them the truth about me, they didn't understand. I'd confess that I was the son of Hermes, the immortal messenger dude with the winged sandals. I'd explain that monsters and Greek gods were real and very much alive in the modern world. My mortal friends would say, "That is so cool! I wish I was a demigod!" Like it's some sort of game. I always ended up leaving.

But Thalia understood. She was like me. Now that I'd found her, I was determined to stick with her. If she wanted to chase a magical glowing goat, then we'd do that, even if I had a bad feeling about it.

We approached the statue. The goat didn't pay us any attention. She chewed some grass then butted her horns against the marble base of the monument. A bronze plaque read: *Robert E. Lee.* I didn't know much about history, but I was pretty sure Lee was a general who lost a war. That didn't strike me as a good omen.

Thalia knelt next to the goat. "Amaltheia?"

The goat turned. She had sad amber eyes and a bronze collar around her neck. Fuzzy white light steamed around her body, but what really caught my attention were her udders. Each teat was labeled with Greek letters, like tattoos. I could read a little Ancient Greek—it was sort of a natural ability for demigods, I guess. The teats read: *Nectar, Milk, Water, Pepsi, Press Here for Ice,* and *Diet Mountain Dew.* Or maybe I read them wrong. I hoped so.

Thalia looked into the goat's eyes. "Amaltheia, what do you want me to do? Did my dad send you?"

The goat glanced at me. She looked a little miffed, like I was intruding on a private conversation.

I took a step back, resisting the urge to grab my weapon. Oh, by the way, my weapon was a golf club. Feel free to laugh. I used to have a sword made from Celestial bronze, which is deadly to monsters, but the sword got melted in acid (long story). Now all I had was a nine-iron that I carried on my back. Not exactly epic. If the goat went commando on us, I'd be in trouble.

I cleared my throat. "Um, Thalia, you sure this goat is from your dad?"

"She's immortal," Thalia said. "When Zeus was a baby, his mom Rhea hid him in a cave—"

"Because Kronos wanted to eat him?" I'd heard that story somewhere, how the old Titan king swallowed his own children.

Thalia nodded. "So this goat, Amaltheia, looked after baby Zeus in his cradle. She nursed him."

"On Diet Mountain Dew?" I asked.

Thalia frowned. "What?"

"Read the udders," I said. "The goat has five flavors plus an ice dispenser."

"Blaaaah," said Amaltheia.

Thalia patted the goat's head. "It's okay. He didn't mean to insult you. Why have you led us here, Amaltheia? Where do you want me to go?"

The goat butted her head against the monument. From above came the sound of creaking metal. I looked up and saw the bronze General Lee move his right arm.

I almost hid behind the goat. Thalia and I had fought several magic moving statues before. They were called automatons, and they were bad news. I wasn't anxious to take on Robert E. Lee with a nine-iron.

Fortunately, the statue didn't attack. He simply pointed across the street.

I gave Thalia a nervous look. "What's that about?"

Thalia nodded in the direction the statue was pointing.

Across the traffic circle stood a red brick mansion overgrown with ivy. On either side, huge oak trees dripped with Spanish moss. The house's windows were shuttered and dark. Peeling white columns flanked the front porch. The door was painted charcoal black. Even on a bright sunny morning, the place looked gloomy and creepy—like a *Gone with the Wind* haunted house.

My mouth felt dry. "The goat wants us to go *there*?"

"Blaah." Amaltheia dipped her head like she was nodding.

Thalia touched the goat's curly horns. "Thank you, Amaltheia. I—I trust you."

I wasn't sure why, considering how afraid Thalia seemed.

The goat bothered me, and not just because she dispensed Pepsi products. Something was nagging at the back of my mind. I thought I'd heard another story about Zeus's goat, something about that glowing fur . . .

Suddenly the mist thickened and swelled around Amaltheia. A miniature storm cloud engulfed her. Lightning flickered through the cloud. When the mist dissolved, the goat was gone.

I hadn't even gotten to try the ice dispenser.

I gazed across the street at the dilapidated house. The mossy trees on either side looked like claws, waiting to grasp us.

"You sure about this?" I asked Thalia.

She turned to me. "Amaltheia leads me to good things. The last time she appeared, she led me to you."

The compliment warmed me like a cup of hot chocolate. I'm a sucker that way. Thalia can flash those blue eyes, give me one kind word, and she can get me to do pretty much whatever. But I couldn't help wondering: back in Charleston, had the goat led her to *me*, or simply led her into a dragon's cave?

I exhaled. "Okay. Creepy mansion, here we come."

The brass door knocker was shaped like Medusa's face, which wasn't a good sign. The porch floorboards creaked under our feet. The windows' shutters were falling apart, but the glass was grimy and covered on the other side with dark curtains, so we couldn't see in.

Thalia knocked.

No answer.

She jiggled the handle, but it seemed to be locked. I was hoping she'd decide to give up. Instead she looked at me expectantly. "Can you do your thing?"

I gritted my teeth. "I hate doing my thing."

Even though I've never met my dad and don't really want to, I share some of his talents. Along with being messenger of the gods, Hermes is the god of merchants—which explains why I'm good with money—and travelers, which explains why the divine jerk left my mom and never came back. He's also the god of thieves. He's stolen things like—oh, Apollo's cattle, women, good ideas, wallets, my mom's sanity, and my chance at a decent life.

Sorry, did that sound bitter?

Anyway, because of my dad's godly thieving, I've got some abilities I don't like to advertise.

I placed my hand on the door's dead bolt. I concentrated, sensing the internal pins that controlled the latch. With a click, the bolt slid back. The lock on the handle was even easier. I tapped it, turned it, and the door swung open.

"That is so cool," Thalia murmured, though she'd seen me do it a dozen times.

The doorway exuded a sour evil smell, like the breath of a dying man. Thalia marched through anyway. I didn't have much choice except to follow.

Inside was an old-fashioned ballroom. High above, a chandelier glowed with trinkets of Celestial bronze—arrowheads, bit of armor, and broken sword hilts—all casting a sickly yellow sheen over the room. Two hallways led off to the left and right. A staircase wrapped around the back wall. Heavy drapes blocked the windows.

The place might've been impressive once, but now it was trashed. The checkerboard marble floor was smeared with mud and crusty dried stuff that I hoped was just ketchup. In one corner, a sofa had been disemboweled. Several mahogany chairs had been busted to kindling. At the base of the stairs sat a heap of cans, rags, and bones—human-sized bones.

Thalia pulled her weapon from her belt. The metal cylinder looked like a Mace canister, but when she flicked it, it expanded until she was holding a full-sized spear with a Celestial bronze point. I grabbed my golf club, which wasn't nearly as cool.

I started to say, "Maybe this isn't such a good—"

The door slammed shut behind us.

I lunged at the handle and pulled. No luck. I pressed my hand on the lock and willed it to open. This time nothing happened.

"Some kind of magic," I said. "We're trapped."

Thalia ran to the nearest window. She tried to part the drapes, but the heavy black fabric wrapped around her hands.

"Luke!" she screamed.

The curtains liquefied into sheets of oily sludge like giant black tongues. They oozed up her arms and covered her spear. It felt like my heart was trying to climb my throat, but I charged at the drapes and whacked them with my golf club.

The ooze shuddered and reverted to fabric long enough for me to pull Thalia free. Her spear clattered on the floor.

I dragged her away as the curtains returned to ooze and tried to catch her. The sheets of sludge lashed at the air. Fortunately, they seemed anchored to the curtain rods. After a few more failed attempts to reach us, the ooze settled down and changed back to drapes.

Thalia shivered in my arms. Her spear lay nearby, smoking as if it had been dipped in acid.

She raised her hands. They were steaming and blistered. Her face paled like she was going into shock.

"Hold on!" I lowered her to the ground and fumbled through my backpack. "Hold on, Thalia. I've got it."

Finally I found my bottle of nectar. The drink of the gods could heal wounds, but the bottle was almost empty. I poured the rest over Thalia's hands. The steam dissipated. The blisters faded.

"You're going to be fine," I said. "Just rest."

"We—we can't . . ." Her voice was shaky, but she managed to stand. She glanced at the drapes with a mixture of fear and nausea. "If all the windows are like that, and the door is locked—"

"We'll find another way out," I promised.

This didn't seem like the time to remind her that we wouldn't have *been* here if not for the stupid goat.

I considered our options: a staircase going up, or two dark hallways. I squinted down the hall to the left. I could make out a pair of small red lights glowing near the floor. Maybe night-lights?

Then the lights moved. They bobbed up and down, growing brighter and closer. A growl made my hair stand on end.

Thalia made a strangled sound. "Um, Luke . . ."

She pointed to the other hallway. Another pair of glowing red eyes glared at us from the shadows. From both hallways came a strange hollow *clack, clack, clack,* like someone playing bone castanets.

"The stairs are looking pretty good," I said.

As if in reply, a man's voice called from somewhere above us: "Yes, this way."

The voice was heavy with sadness, as if he were giving directions to a funeral.

"Who are you?" I shouted.

"Hurry," the voice called down, but he didn't sound excited about it.

To my right, the same voice echoed, "Hurry." *Clack, clack, clack.*

I did a double take. The voice seemed to have come from the thing in the hallway—the thing with the glowing red eyes. But how could one voice come from two different places?

Then the same voice called out from the hallway on the left: "Hurry." *Clack, clack, clack.*

Now I've faced some scary stuff before—fire-breathing dogs, pit scorpions, dragons—not to mention a set of oily black man-eating draperies. But something about those voices echoing all around me, those glowing eyes advancing from either direction, and the weird clacking noises made me feel like a deer surrounded by wolves. Every muscle in my body tensed. My instincts said, *Run.*

I grabbed Thalia's hand and bolted for the stairs.

"Luke—"

"Come on!"

"If it's another trap—"

"No choice!"

I bounded up the stairs, dragging Thalia with me. I knew she was right. We might be running straight to our deaths, but I also knew we had to get away from those things downstairs.

I was afraid to look back, but I could hear the creatures closing—snarling like wildcats, pounding across the marble floor with a sound like horse's hooves. What in Hades *were* they?

At the top of the stairs, we plunged down another hallway. Dimly flickering wall sconces made the doors along either side seem to dance. I jumped over a pile of bones, accidentally kicking a human skull.

Somewhere ahead of us, the man's voice called, "This way!" He sounded more urgent than before. "Last door on the left! Hurry!"

Behind us, the creatures echoed his words: "Left! Hurry!"

Maybe the creatures were just mimicking like parrots. Or maybe the voice in front of us belonged to a monster too. Still, something about the man's tone *felt* real. He sounded alone and miserable, like a hostage.

"We have to help him," Thalia announced, as if reading my thoughts.

"Yeah," I agreed.

We charged ahead. The corridor became more dilapidated—wallpaper peeling away like tree bark, light sconces smashed to pieces. The carpet was ripped to shreds and littered with bones. Light seeped from underneath the last door on the left.

Behind us, the pounding of hooves got louder.

We reached the door and I launched myself against it, but it opened on its own. Thalia and I spilled inside, face-planting on the carpet.

The door slammed shut.

Outside, the creatures growled in frustration and scraped against the walls.

"Hello," said the man's voice, much closer now. "I'm very sorry."

My head was spinning. I thought I'd heard him off to my left, but when I looked up, he was standing right in front of us.

He wore snakeskin boots and a mottled green-and-brown suit that might've been made from the same material. He was tall and gaunt, with spiky gray hair almost as wild as Thalia's. He looked like a very old, sickly, fashionably dressed Einstein.

His shoulders slumped. His sad green eyes were underscored

with bags. He might've been handsome once, but the skin of his face hung loose as if he'd been partially deflated.

His room was arranged like a studio apartment. Unlike the rest of the house, it was in fairly good shape. Against the far wall was a twin bed, a desk with a computer, and a window covered with dark drapes like the ones downstairs. Along the right wall stood a bookcase, a small kitchenette, and two doorways—one leading into a bathroom, the other into a large closet.

Thalia said, "Um, Luke . . ."

She pointed to our left.

My heart almost burst out of my rib cage.

The left side of the room had a row of iron bars like a prison cell. Inside was the scariest zoo exhibit I'd ever seen. A gravel floor was littered with bones and pieces of armor, and prowling back and forth was a monster with a lion's body and rust-red fur. Instead of paws it had hooves like a horse, and its tail lashed around like a bullwhip. Its head was a mixture of horse and wolf—with pointed ears, an elongated snout, and black lips that looked disturbingly human.

The monster snarled. For a second I thought it was wearing one of those mouth guards that boxers use. Instead of teeth, it had two solid horseshoe-shaped plates of bone. When it snapped its mouth, the bone plates made the jarring *clack, clack, clack* I'd heard downstairs.

The monster fixed its glowing red eyes on me. Saliva dripped from its weird bony ridges. I wanted to run, but there was nowhere to go. I could still hear the other creatures—at least two of them—growling out in the hallway.

Thalia helped me to my feet. I gripped her hand and faced the old man.

"Who are you?" I demanded. "What's that thing in the cage?"

The old man grimaced. His expression was so full of misery I thought he might cry. He opened his mouth, but when he spoke, the words didn't come from him.

Like some horrific ventriloquist act, the monster spoke for him, in the voice of an old man: "I am Halcyon Green. I'm terribly sorry, but *you* are in the cage. You've been lured here to die."

———

We'd left Thalia's spear downstairs, so we had just one weapon—my golf club. I brandished it at the old man, but he made no threatening moves. He looked so pitiful and depressed I couldn't bring myself to smack him.

"Y-you'd better explain," I stammered. "Why—how—what . . . ?"

As you can tell, I'm good with words.

Behind the bars, the monster clacked its bone-plated jaws.

"I understand your confusion," it said in the old man's voice. Its sympathetic tone didn't match the homicidal glow in its eyes.

"The creature you see here is a leucrota. It has a talent for imitating human voices. That is how it lures its prey."

I looked back and forth from the man to the monster. "But . . . the voice is yours? I mean, the dude in the snakeskin suit—I'm hearing what *he* wants to say?"

"That is correct." The leucrota sighed heavily. "I am, as you say, the dude in the snakeskin suit. Such is my curse. My name is Halcyon Green, son of Apollo."

Thalia stumbled backward. "You're a *demigod*? But you're so—"

"Old?" the leucrota asked. The man, Halcyon Green, studied his liver-spotted hands, as if he couldn't believe they were his. "Yes, I am."

I understood Thalia's surprise. We'd only met a few other demigods in our travels—some friendly, some not so much. But they'd all been kids like us. Our lives were so dangerous, Thalia and I figured it was unlikely any demigod could live to be an adult. Yet Halcyon Green was *ancient*, like sixty at least.

"How long have you been here?" I asked.

Halcyon shrugged listlessly. The monster spoke for him: "I have lost count. Decades? Because my father is the god of oracles, I was born with the curse of seeing the future. Apollo warned me to keep quiet. He told me I should never share what I saw because it would anger the gods. But many years ago . . . I simply had to speak. I met a young girl who was destined to die in an accident. I saved her life by telling her the future."

I tried to focus on the old man, but it was hard not to look at the monster's mouth—those black lips, the slavering bone-plated jaws.

"I don't get it . . ." I forced myself to meet Halcyon's eyes. "You did something good. Why would that anger the gods?"

"They don't like mortals meddling with fate," the leucrota said. "My father cursed me. He forced me to wear these clothes, the skin of Python, who once guarded the Oracle of Delphi, as a reminder that I was *not* an oracle. He took away my voice and locked me in this mansion, my boyhood home. Then the gods set the leucrotae to guard me. Normally, leucrotae only mimic human speech, but these are linked to my thoughts. They speak for me. They keep me alive as bait, to lure other demigods. It was Apollo's way of reminding me, forever, that my voice would only lead others to their doom."

An angry coppery taste filled my mouth. I already knew the gods could be cruel. My deadbeat dad had ignored me for fourteen years. But Halcyon Green's curse was just plain *wrong*. It was evil.

"You should fight back," I said. "You didn't deserve this. Break out. Kill the monsters. We'll help you."

"He's right," Thalia said. "That's Luke, by the way. I'm Thalia. We've fought plenty of monsters. There has to be something we can do, Halcyon."

"Call me Hal," the leucrota said. The old man shook his head dejectedly. "But you don't understand. You're not the first to come here. I'm afraid all the demigods feel there's hope when they first arrive. Sometimes I try to help them. It never works. The windows are guarded by deadly drapes—"

"I noticed," Thalia muttered.

"—and the door is heavily enchanted. It will let you in, but not out."

"We'll see about that." I turned and pressed my hand to the lock. I concentrated until sweat trickled down my neck, but nothing happened. My powers were useless.

"I told you," the leucrota said bitterly. "None of us can leave. Fighting the monsters is hopeless. They can't be hurt by any metal known to man or god."

To prove his point, the old man brushed aside the edge of his snakeskin jacket, revealed a dagger on his belt. He unsheathed the wicked-looking Celestial bronze blade and approached the monster's cell.

The leucrota snarled at him. Hal jabbed his knife between the bars, straight at the monster's head. Normally, Celestial bronze would disintegrate a monster with one hit. The blade simply glanced off the leucrota's snout, leaving no mark. The leucrota kicked its hooves at the bars, and Hal backed away.

"You see?" the monster spoke for Hal.

"So you just give up?" Thalia demanded. "You help the monsters lure us in and wait for them to kill us?"

Hal sheathed his dagger. "I'm so sorry, my dear, but I have little choice. I'm trapped here, too. If I don't cooperate, the monsters let me starve. The monsters could have killed you the moment you entered the house, but they use me to lure you upstairs. They allow me your company for a while. It eases my loneliness. And then . . . well, the monsters like to eat at sundown. Today, that will be at 7:03." He gestured to a digital clock on his desk, which read *10:34 AM.* "After you are gone, I—I subsist on whatever rations you carried."

He glanced hungrily at my backpack, and a shiver went down my spine.

"You're as bad as the monsters," I said.

The old man winced. I didn't care much if I hurt his feelings. In my backpack I had two Snickers bars, a ham sandwich, a canteen of water, and an empty bottle for nectar. I didn't want to get killed for that.

"You're right to hate me," the leucrota said in Hal's voice, "but I can't save you. At sunset, those bars will rise. The monsters will drag you away and kill you. There is no escape."

Inside the monster's enclosure, a square panel on the back wall ground open. I hadn't even noticed the panel before, but it must have led to another room. Two more leucrotae stalked into the cage. All three fixed their glowing red eyes on me, their bony mouth-plates snapping with anticipation.

I wondered how the monsters could eat with such strange mouths. As if to answer my question, a leucrota picked up an old piece of armor in its mouth. The Celestial bronze breastplate looked thick enough to stop a spear-thrust, but the leucrota clamped down with the force of a vise grip and bit a horseshoe-shaped hole in the metal.

"As you see," said another leucrota in Hal's voice, "the monsters are remarkably strong."

My legs felt like soggy spaghetti. Thalia's fingers dug into my arm.

"Send them away," she pleaded. "Hal, can you make them leave?"

The old man frowned. The first monster said: "If I do that, we won't be able to talk."

The second monster picked up in the same voice: "Besides, any escape strategy you can think of, someone else has already tried."

The third monster said: "There is no point in private talks."

Thalia paced, as restless as the monsters. "Do they know what we're saying? I mean, do they just speak, or do they understand the words?"

The first leucrota made a high-pitched whine. Then it imitated Thalia's voice: "Do they understand the words?"

My stomach churned. The monster had mimicked Thalia

perfectly. If I'd heard that voice in the dark, calling for help, I would've run straight toward it.

The second monster spoke for Hal: "The creatures are intelligent, the way dogs are intelligent. They comprehend emotions and a few simple phrases. They can lure their prey by crying things like 'Help!' But I'm not sure how much human speech they really understand. It doesn't matter. You can't fool them."

"Send them away," I said. "You have a computer. Type what you want to say. If we're going to die at sunset, I don't want those things staring at me all day."

Hal hesitated. Then he turned to the monsters and stared at them in silence. After a few moments, the leucrotae snarled. They stalked out of the enclosure and the back panel closed behind them.

Hal looked at me. He spread his hands as if apologizing, or asking a question.

"Luke," Thalia said anxiously, "do you have a plan?"

"Not yet," I admitted. "But we'd better come up with one by sunset."

It was an odd feeling, waiting to die. Normally when Thalia and I fought monsters, we had about two seconds to figure out a plan. The threat was immediate. We lived or died instantly. Now we had all day trapped in a room with nothing to do, knowing that at sunset those cage bars would rise and we'd be trampled to death and torn apart by monsters that couldn't be killed with any weapon. Then Halcyon Green would eat my Snickers bars.

The suspense was almost worse than an attack.

Part of me was tempted to knock out the old man with my golf club and feed him to his drapes. Then at least he couldn't help the monsters lure any more demigods to their deaths. But I couldn't make myself do it. Hal was so frail and pathetic. Besides, his curse wasn't his fault. He'd been trapped in this room for decades, forced to depend on monsters for his voice and his survival, forced to watch other demigods die, all because he'd saved a girl's life. What kind of justice was that?

I was still angry with Hal for luring us here, but I could understand why he'd lost hope after so many years. If anybody deserved a golf club across the head, it was Apollo—and *all* the other deadbeat parent Olympian gods, for that matter.

We took inventory of Hal's prison apartment. The bookshelves were stuffed with everything from ancient history to thriller novels.

You're welcome to read anything, Hal typed on his computer. *Just please not my diary. It's personal.*

He put his hand protectively on a battered green leather book next to his keyboard.

"No problem," I said. I doubted any of the books would help us, and I couldn't imagine Hal had anything interesting to write about in his diary, being stuck in this room most of his life.

He showed us the computer's Internet browser. Great. We could order pizza and watch the monsters eat the delivery guy. Not very helpful. I suppose we could've e-mailed someone for help, except we didn't have anyone to contact, and I'd never used e-mail. Thalia and I didn't even carry phones. We'd found out the hard way that when demigods use technology, it attracts monsters like blood attracts sharks.

We moved on to the bathroom. It was pretty clean considering how long Hal had lived here. He had two spare sets of snake-skin clothes, apparently just hand-washed, hanging from the rod above the bathtub. His medicine cabinet was stocked with scavenged supplies—toiletries, medicines, toothbrushes, first-aid gear, ambrosia, and nectar. I tried not to think about where all this had come from as I searched but didn't see anything that could defeat the leucrotae.

Thalia slammed a drawer shut in frustration. "I don't understand! Why did Amaltheia bring me here? Did the other demigods come here because of the goat?"

Hal frowned. He motioned for us to follow him back to his computer. He hunched over the keyboard and typed: *What goat?*

I didn't see any point in keeping it a secret. I told him how we'd followed Zeus's glowing Pepsi-dispensing goat into Richmond, and how she had pointed us to this house.

Hal looked baffled. He typed: *I've heard of Amaltheia, but don't know why she would bring you here. The other demigods were attracted to the mansion because of the treasure. I assumed you were, too.*

"Treasure?" Thalia asked.

Hal got up and showed us his walk-in closet. It was full of more supplies collected from unfortunate demigods—coats much too small for Hal, some old-fashioned wood-and-pitch torches, dented pieces of armor, and a few Celestial bronze swords that were bent and broken. Such a waste. I needed another sword.

Hal rearranged boxes of books, shoes, a few bars of gold, and a small basket full of diamonds that he didn't seem interested in. He unearthed a two-foot-square metal floor safe and gestured at it like: *Ta-da.*

"Can you open it?" I asked.

Hal shook his head.

"Do you know what's inside?" Thalia asked.

Again, Hal shook his head.

"It's trapped," I guessed.

Hal nodded emphatically, then traced a finger across his neck.

I knelt next to the safe. I didn't touch it, but I held my hands close to the combination lock. My fingers tingled with warmth as if the box were a hot oven. I concentrated until I could sense the mechanisms inside. I didn't like what I found.

"This thing is bad news," I muttered. "Whatever's inside must be important."

Thalia knelt next to me. "Luke, this is why we're here." Her voice was full of excitement. "Zeus wanted me to find this."

I looked at her skeptically. I didn't know how she could have such faith in her dad. Zeus hadn't treated her any better than Hermes treated me. Besides, a lot of demigods had been led here. All of them were dead.

Still, she fixed me with those intense blue eyes, and I knew this was another time Thalia would get her way.

I sighed. "You're going to ask me to open it, aren't you?"

"Can you?"

I chewed my lip. Maybe next time I teamed up with someone, I should choose someone I didn't like so much. I just couldn't say no to Thalia.

"People have tried to open this before," I warned. "There's a curse on the handle. I'm guessing whoever touches it gets burned to a pile of ashes."

I looked up at Hal. His face turned as gray as his hair. I took that as a confirmation.

"Can you bypass the curse?" Thalia asked me.

"I think so," I said. "But it's the second trap I'm worried about."

"The second trap?" she asked.

"Nobody's managed to trigger the combination," I said. "I know that because there's a poison canister ready to break as soon as you hit the third number. It's never been activated."

Judging from Hal's wide eyes, this was news to him.

"I can try to disable it," I said, "but if I mess up, this whole apartment is going to fill with gas. We'll die."

Thalia swallowed. "I trust you. Just . . . don't mess up."

I turned to the old man. "You could maybe hide in the bathtub. Put some wet towels over your face. It might protect you."

Hal shifted uneasily. The snakeskin fabric of his suit rippled as if it was still alive, trying to swallow something unpleasant. Emotions played across his face—fear, doubt, but mostly shame. I guess he couldn't stand the idea of cowering in a bathtub while two kids risked their lives. Or maybe there was a little demigod spirit left in him after all. He gestured at the safe like: *Go ahead.*

I touched the combination lock. I concentrated so hard I felt like I was dead-lifting five hundred pounds. My pulse quickened. A line of sweat trickled down my nose. Finally I felt gears turning. Metal groaned, tumblers clicked, and the bolts popped back. Carefully avoiding the handle, I pried open the door with my fingertips and extracted an unbroken vial of green liquid.

Hal exhaled.

Thalia kissed me on the cheek, which she probably shouldn't have done while I was holding a tube of deadly poison.

"You are *so* good," she said.

Did that make the risk worth it? Yeah, pretty much.

I looked into the safe, and some of my enthusiasm faded. "That's *it*?"

Thalia reached in and pulled out a bracelet.

It didn't look like much, just a row of polished silver links.

Thalia latched it around her wrist. Nothing happened.

She scowled. "It should *do* something. If Zeus sent me here—"

Hal clapped his hands to get our attention. Suddenly his eyes looked almost as crazy as his hair. He gesticulated wildly, but I had no idea what he was trying to say. Finally he stamped his snakeskin boot in frustration and led us back to the main room.

He sat at his computer and started to type. I glanced at the clock on his desk. Maybe time traveled faster in the house, or maybe time just flies when you're waiting to die, but it was already past noon. Our day was half over.

Hal showed us the short novel he'd written: *You're the ones!! You actually got the treasure!! I can't believe it!! That safe has been sealed since before I was born!! Apollo told me my curse would end when the owner of the treasure claimed it!! If you're the owner—*

There was more, with plenty more exclamation points, but before I could finish reading, Thalia said, "Hold it. I've never seen this bracelet. How could I be the owner? And if your curse is supposed to end now, does that mean the monsters are gone?"

A *clack, clack, clack* from the hallway answered that question.

I frowned at Hal. "Do you have your voice back?"

He opened his mouth, but no sound came out. His shoulders slumped.

"Maybe Apollo meant we're going to rescue you," Thalia said.

Hal typed a new sentence: *Or maybe I die today.*

"Thank you, Mr. Cheerful," I said. "I thought *you* could tell the future. You don't know what will happen?"

Hal typed: *I can't look. It's too dangerous. You can see what happened to me last time I tried to use my powers.*

"Sure," I grumbled. "Don't take the risk. You might mess up this nice life you've got here."

I knew that was mean. But the old man's cowardice annoyed me. He'd let the gods use him as a punching bag for too long. It was time he fought back, preferably before Thalia and I became the leucrotae's next meal.

Hal lowered his head. His chest was shaking, and I realized he was crying silently.

Thalia shot me an irritated look. "It's okay, Hal. We're not giving up. This bracelet must be the answer. It's got to have a special power."

Hal took a shaky breath. He turned to his keyboard and typed: *It's silver. Even if it turns into a weapon, the monsters can't be hurt by any metal.*

Thalia turned to me with a silent plea in her eyes, like: *Your turn for a helpful idea.*

I studied the empty enclosure, the metal panel through which the monsters had exited. If the apartment door wouldn't open again, and the window was covered by man-eating acid drapes, then that panel might be our only exit. We couldn't use metal weapons. I had a vial of poison, but if I was right about that stuff, it would kill everyone in the room as soon as it dispersed. I ran through another dozen ideas in my head, quickly rejecting them all.

"We'll have to find a different kind of weapon," I decided. "Hal, let me borrow your computer."

Hal looked doubtful, but he gave me his seat.

I stared at the screen. Honestly, I'd never used computers much. Like I said, technology attracts monsters. But Hermes *was* the god of communication, roadways, and commerce. Maybe that meant he had some power over the Internet. I could really use a divine Google hit right about now.

"Just once," I muttered to the screen, "cut me some slack. Show me there's an upside to being your son."

"What, Luke?" Thalia asked.

"Nothing," I said.

I opened the Web browser and started typing. I looked up leucrotae, hoping to find their weaknesses. The Internet had almost nothing on them, except that they were legendary animals that lured their prey by imitating human voices.

I searched for "Greek weapons." I found some great images of swords, spears, and catapults, but I doubted we could kill monsters with low-resolution JPEGs. I typed in a list of things we had in the room—torches, Celestial bronze, poison, Snickers bars, golf club—hoping that some sort of magic formula would pop up for a leucrota death ray. No such luck. I typed in "Help me kill leucrotae." The closest hit I got was *Help me cure leukemia.*

My head was throbbing. I didn't have any concept of how long I'd been searching until looked at the clock: four in the afternoon. How was that *possible*?

Meanwhile, Thalia had been trying to activate her new bracelet, with no luck. She'd twisted it, tapped it, shaken it, worn it on her ankle, thrown it against the wall, and swung it over her head yelling "Zeus!" Nothing happened.

We looked at each other, and I knew we were both out of ideas. I thought about what Hal Green had told us. All demigods started off hopeful. All of them had ideas for escape. All of them failed.

I couldn't let that happen. Thalia and I had survived too much to give up now. But for the life of me (and I mean that literally) I couldn't think of anything else to try.

Hal walked over and gestured at the keyboard.

"Go ahead," I said dejectedly.

We changed places.

Running out of time, he typed. *I'll try to read the future.*

Thalia frowned. "I thought you said that was too dangerous."

It doesn't matter, Hal typed. *Luke is right. I'm a cowardly old man, but Apollo can't punish me any worse than he already has. Perhaps I'll see something that will help you. Thalia, give me your hands.*

He turned to her.

Thalia hesitated.

Outside the apartment, the leucrotae growled and scraped against the corridor. They sounded hungry.

Thalia placed her hands in Halcyon Green's. The old man closed his eyes and concentrated, the same way I do when I'm reading a complicated lock.

He winced, then took a shaky breath. He looked up at Thalia with an expression of sympathy. He turned to the keyboard and hesitated a long time before starting to type.

You are destined to survive today, Hal typed.

"That's—that's good, right?" she asked. "Why do you look so sad?"

Hal stared at the blinking cursor. He typed, *Someday soon, you will sacrifice yourself to save your friends. I see things that are . . . hard to describe. Years of solitude. You will stand tall and still, alive but sleeping. You will change once, and then change again. Your path will be sad and lonely. But someday you will find your family again.*

Thalia clenched her fists. She started to speak, then paced the room. Finally she slammed her palm against the bookshelves. "That doesn't make any *sense.* I'll sacrifice myself, but I'll live. Changing, sleeping? You call that a future? I—I don't even *have* a family. Just my mom, and there's no way I'm going back to her."

Hal pursed his lips. He typed, *I'm sorry. I don't control what I see. But I didn't mean your mother.*

Thalia almost backed up into the drapes. She caught herself just in time, but she looked dizzy, as if she'd just stepped off a roller coaster.

"Thalia?" I asked, as gently as I could. "Do you know what he's talking about?"

She gave me a cornered look. I didn't understand why she seemed so rattled. I knew she didn't like to talk about her life back in L.A., but she'd told me she was an only child, and she'd never mentioned any relatives beside her mom.

"It's nothing," she said at last. "Forget it. Hal's fortune-telling skills are rusty."

I'm pretty sure not even Thalia believed that.

"Hal," I said, "there's got to be more. You told us that Thalia will survive. *How?* Did you see anything about the bracelet? Or the goat? We need *something* that will help."

He shook his head sadly. He typed, *I saw nothing about the bracelet. I'm sorry. I know a little about Amaltheia the goat, but I doubt it will help. The goat nursed Zeus when he was a baby. Later, Zeus slew her and used her skin to make his shield—the aegis.*

I scratched my chin. I was pretty sure that was the story I'd been trying to remember earlier about the goat's hide. It seemed important, though I couldn't figure out why. "So Zeus killed his own mama goat. Typical god thing to do. Thalia, you know anything about the shield?"

She nodded, clearly relieved to change the subject. "Athena put the head of Medusa on the front of it and had the whole thing covered in Celestial bronze. She and Zeus took turns using it in battle. It would frighten away their enemies."

I didn't see how the information could help. Obviously, the goat Amaltheia had come back to life. That happened a lot with mythological monsters—they eventually re-formed from the pit of Tartarus. But why had Amaltheia led us here?

A bad thought occurred to me. If *I'd* been skinned by Zeus, I definitely wouldn't be interested in helping him anymore. In fact, I might have a vendetta against Zeus's children. Maybe that's why Amaltheia had brought us to the mansion.

Hal Green held out his hands to me. His grim expression told me it was my turn for a fortune-telling.

A wave of dread washed over me. After hearing Thalia's future, I didn't want to know mine. What if she survived, and I didn't? What if we both survived, but Thalia sacrificed herself to save me somewhere down the line, like Hal had mentioned? I couldn't bear that.

"Don't, Luke," Thalia said bitterly. "The gods were right. Hal's prophecies don't help anybody."

The old man blinked his watery eyes. His hands were so frail, it was hard to believe he carried the blood of an immortal god. He had told us his curse would end today, one way or another. He'd foreseen Thalia surviving. If he saw anything in my future that would help, I had to try.

I gave him my hands.

Hal took a deep breath and closed his eyes. His snakeskin jacket glistened as if it were trying to shed. I forced myself to stay calm.

I could feel Hal's pulse in my fingers—one, two, three.

His eyes flew open. He yanked his hands away and stared at me in terror.

"Okay," I said. My tongue felt like sandpaper. "I'm guessing you didn't see anything good."

Hal turned to his computer. He stared at the screen so long I thought he'd gone into a trance.

Finally he typed, *Fire. I saw fire.*

Thalia frowned. "Fire? You mean today? Is that going to help us?"

Hal looked up miserably. He nodded.

"There's more," I pressed. "What scared you so badly?"

He avoided my eyes. Reluctantly he typed, *Hard to be sure. Luke, I also saw a sacrifice in your future. A choice. But also a betrayal.*

I waited. Hal didn't elaborate.

"A betrayal," Thalia said. Her tone was dangerous. "You mean someone betrays Luke? Because Luke would never betray anyone."

Hal typed, *His path is hard to see. But if he survives today, he will betray—*

Thalia grabbed the keyboard. "Enough! You lure demigods here, then you take away their hope with your horrible predictions? No wonder the others gave up—just like you gave up. You're pathetic!"

Anger kindled in Hal's eyes. I didn't think the old man had it in him, but he rose to his feet. For a moment, I thought he might lunge at Thalia.

"Go ahead," Thalia growled. "Take a swing, old man. You have any fire left?"

"Stop it!" I ordered. Hal Green immediately backed down. I could swear the old man was terrified of me now, but I didn't want to know what he saw in his visions. Whatever nightmares were in my future, I had to survive today first.

"Fire," I said. "You mentioned fire."

He nodded, then spread his hands to indicate he had no further details.

An idea buzzed in the back of my head. Fire. Greek weapons. Some of the supplies we had in this apartment . . . the list I'd put into the search engine, hoping for a magic formula.

"What is it?" Thalia asked. "I know that look. You're on to something."

"Let me see the keyboard." I sat at the computer and did a new Web search.

An article popped up immediately.

Thalia peered over my shoulder. "Luke, that would be perfect! But I thought that stuff was just a legend."

"I don't know," I admitted. "If it's real, how do we make it? There's no recipe here."

Hal wrapped his knuckles on the desk to get our attention. His face was animated. He pointed at his bookshelves.

"Ancient history books," Thalia said. "Hal's right. A lot of those are really old. They probably have information that wouldn't be on the Internet."

All three of us ran to the shelves. We started pulling out books. Soon Hal's library looked like it had been hit by a hurricane, but the old man didn't seem to care. He tossed titles and flipped through pages as fast as we did. In fact, without him, we never would've found the answer. After lots of fruitless searching, he came racing over, tapping a page in an old leather-bound book.

I scanned the list of ingredients, and my excitement built. "This is it. The recipe for Greek fire."

How had I known to search for it? Perhaps my dad, Hermes, the jack-of-all-trades god, was guiding me, since he's got a way with potions and alchemy. Perhaps I'd seen the recipe somewhere before, and searching the apartment had triggered that memory.

Everything we needed was in this room. I'd seen all of the ingredients when we'd gone through the supplies from defeated demigods: pitch from the old torches, a bottle of godly nectar, alcohol from Hal's first-aid kit . . .

Actually, I shouldn't write down the whole recipe, even in this diary. If someone came across it and learned the secret of Greek fire . . . well, I don't want to be responsible for burning down the mortal world.

I read to the end of the list. There was only one thing missing.

"A catalyst." I looked at Thalia. "We need lightning."

Her eyes widened. "Luke, I can't. Last time—"

Hal dragged us to the computer and typed, *You can summon lightning????*

"Sometimes," Thalia admitted. "It's a Zeus thing. But I can't do it indoors. And even if we were outside, I'd have trouble controlling the strike. Last time, I almost killed Luke."

The hairs on my neck stood up as I remembered that accident.

"It'll be fine." I tried to sound confident. "I'll prepare the mixture. When it's ready, there's an outlet under the computer. You can call down a lightning strike on the house and blast it through the electrical wiring."

"And set the house on fire," Thalia added.

Hal typed, *You'll do that anyway if you succeed. You <u>do</u> understand how dangerous Greek fire is?*

I swallowed. "Yeah. It's magical fire. Whatever it touches, it burns. You can't put it out with water, or a fire extinguisher, or anything else. But if we can make enough for some kind of bomb and throw it at the leucrotae—"

"They'll burn." Thalia glanced at the old man. "Please tell me the monsters aren't immune to fire."

Hal knit his eyebrows. *I don't think so*, he typed. *But Greek fire will turn this room into an inferno. It will spread through the entire house in a matter of seconds.*

I looked at the empty enclosure. According to Hal's clock, we had roughly an hour before sunset. When those bars rose and the leucrotae attacked, we might have a chance—if we could surprise the monsters with an explosion, and if we could somehow get around them and reach the escape panel at the back of the cage without getting eaten or burned alive. Too many ifs.

My mind ran through a dozen different strategies, but I kept coming back to what Hal had said about *sacrifice*. I couldn't escape the feeling there was no way all three of us could get out alive.

"Let's make the Greek fire," I said. "Then we'll figure out the rest."

Thalia and Hal helped me gather the things we needed. We started Hal's stovetop and did some extremely dangerous cooking. Time passed too quickly. Outside in the hallway, the leucrotae growled and clacked their jaws.

The drapes on the window blocked out all sunlight, but the clock told us we were almost out of time.

My face beaded with sweat as I mixed the ingredients. Every time I blinked, I remembered Hal's words on that computer screen, as if they'd been burned onto the back of my eyes: *A sacrifice in your future. A choice. But also a betrayal.*

What did he mean? I was sure he hadn't told me everything. But one thing was clear: My future terrified him.

I tried to focus on my work. I didn't really know what I was doing, but I had no choice. Maybe Hermes was watching out for me, lending me some of his alchemy know-how. Or maybe I just got lucky. Finally I had a pot full of goopy black gunk, which I poured into an old glass jelly jar. I sealed the lid.

"There." I handed the jar to Thalia. "Can you zap it? The glass should keep it from exploding until we break the jar."

Thalia didn't look thrilled. "I'll try. I'll have to expose some wiring in the wall. And to summon the lightning, that'll take a few minutes of concentration. You guys should probably step back, in case . . . you know, I explode or something."

She grabbed a screwdriver from Hal's kitchen drawer, crawled under the computer desk, and stared tinkering with the outlet.

Hal picked up his green leather diary. He gestured for me to follow him. We walked to the closet doorway, where Hal took a pen from his jacket and flipped through the book. I saw pages and pages of neat, cramped handwriting. Finally Hal found an empty page and scribbled something.

He handed the book to me.

The note read, *Luke, I want you to take this diary. It has my predictions, my notes about the future, my thoughts about where I went wrong. I think it might help you.*

I shook my head. "Hal, this is yours. Keep it."

He took back the book and wrote, *You have an important future. Your choices will change the world. You can learn from my mistakes, continue the diary. It might help you with your decisions.*

"What decisions?" I asked. "What did you see that scared you so badly?"

His pen hovered over the page for a long time. *I think I finally understand why I was cursed*, he wrote. *Apollo was right. Sometimes the future really is better left a mystery.*

"Hal, your father was a jerk. You didn't deserve—"

Hal tapped the page insistently. He scribbled, *Just promise me you'll keep up with the diary. If I'd started recording my thoughts earlier in my life, I might have avoided some stupid mistakes. And one more thing—*

He set the pen in his diary and unclipped the Celestial bronze dagger from his belt. He offered it to me.

"I can't," I told him. "I mean, I appreciate it, but I'm more of a sword guy. And besides, you're coming with us. You'll need that weapon."

He shook his head and put the dagger into my hands. He returned to writing: *That blade was a gift from the girl I saved. She promised me it would always protect its owner.*

Hal took a shaky breath. He must've known how bitterly ironic that promise sounded, given his curse. He wrote, *A dagger doesn't have the power or reach of a sword, but it can be an excellent weapon in the right hands. I'll feel better knowing you have it.*

He met my eyes, and I finally understood what he was planning.

"Don't," I said. "We can all make it out."

Hal pursed his lips. He wrote, *We both know that's impossible. I can communicate with the leucrotae. I am the logical choice for bait. You and Thalia wait in the closet. I'll lure the monsters into the bathroom. I'll buy you a few seconds to reach the exit panel before I set off the explosion. It's the only way you'll have time.*

"No," I said.

But his expression was grim and determined. He didn't look like a cowardly old man anymore. He looked like a demigod, ready to go out fighting.

I couldn't believe he was offering to sacrifice his life for two kids he'd just met, especially after he'd suffered for so many years. And yet, I didn't need pen and paper to see what he was thinking. This was his chance at redemption. He would do one last heroic thing, and his curse would end today, just as Apollo had foreseen.

He scribbled something and handed me the diary. The last word read: *Promise.*

I took a deep breath, and closed the book. "Yeah. I promise."

Thunder shook the house. We both jumped. Over at the computer desk, something went *ZZZAP-POP!* White smoke billowed from the computer, and a smell like burning tires filled the room.

Thalia sat up grinning. The wall behind her was blistered and blackened. The electrical outlet had completely melted, but in her hands, the jelly jar of Greek fire was now glowing green.

"Someone order a magic bomb?" she asked.

Just then, the clock registered 7:03. The enclosure's bars began to rise, and the panel at the back started to open.

We were out of time.

———

The old man held out his hand.

"Thalia," I said. "Give Hal the Greek fire."

She looked back and forth between us. "But—"

"He has to." My voice sounded more gravelly than usual. "He's going to help us escape."

As the meaning of my words dawned on her, her face blanched. "Luke, no."

The bars had risen halfway to the ceiling. The trapdoor ground open slowly. A red hoof thrust its way through the crack. Inside the chute, the leucrotae growled and clacked their jaws.

"There's no time," I warned. "Come on!"

Hal took the jar of fire from Thalia. He gave her a brave smile, then nodded to me. I remembered the final word he'd written: *Promise.*

I slipped his diary and dagger into my pack. Then I pulled Thalia into the closet with me.

A split second later, we heard the leucrotae burst into the room. All three of the monsters hissed and growled and trampled across the furniture, anxious to feed.

"In here!" Hal's voice called. It must've been one of the monsters speaking for him, but his words sound brave and confident. "I've got them trapped in the bathroom! Come on, you ugly mutts!"

It was strange hearing a leucrota insult itself, but the ploy seemed to work. The creatures galloped toward the bathroom.

I gripped Thalia's hand. "Now."

We burst out of the closet and sprinted for the enclosure. Inside, the panel was already closing. One of the leucrotae snarled in surprise and turned to follow us, but I didn't dare look back. We scrambled into the cage. I lunged for the exit panel, wedging it open with my golf club.

"Go, go, go!" I yelled.

Thalia wriggled through as the metal plate started to bend the golf club.

From the bathroom, Hal's voice yelled, "You know what this is, you Tartarus scum dogs? This is your last meal!"

The leucrota landed on me. I twisted, screaming, as its bony mouth snapped at the air where my face had just been.

I managed to punch its snout, but it was like hitting a bag of wet cement.

Then something grabbed my arm. Thalia pulled me into the chute. The panel closed, snapping my golf club.

We crawled through a metal duct into another bedroom and stumbled for the door.

I heard Halcyon Green, shouting a battle cry: "For Apollo!"

And the mansion shook with a massive explosion.

We burst into the hallway, which was already on fire. Flames licked the wallpaper and the carpet steamed. Hal's bedroom door had been blown off its hinges, and fire was pouring out like an avalanche, vaporizing everything in its path.

We reached the stairs. The smoke was so thick, I couldn't see the bottom. We stumbled and coughed, the heat searing my eyes and my lungs. We got to the base of the stairs, and I was beginning to think we'd reach the door, when the leucrota pounced, knocking me flat on my back.

It must have been the one that followed us into the enclosure. I suppose it had been far enough away from the explosion to survive the initial blast and had somehow escaped the bedroom, though it didn't look like it had enjoyed the experience. Its red fur was singed black. Its pointed ears were on fire, and one of its glowing red eyes was swollen shut.

"Luke!" Thalia screamed. She grabbed her spear, which had been lying on the ballroom floor all day, and rammed the point against the monster's ribs, but that only annoyed the leucrota.

It snapped its bone-plated jaws at her, keeping one hoof planted on my chest. I couldn't move, and I knew the beast could crush my chest by applying even the slightest extra pressure.

My eyes stung from the smoke. I could hardly breathe. I saw Thalia try to spear the monster again, and a flash of metal caught my eye—the silver bracelet.

Something finally clicked in my mind: the story of Amaltheia the goat, who'd led us here. Thalia had been destined to find that treasure. It belonged to the child of Zeus.

"Thalia!" I gasped. "The shield! What was it called?"

"What shield?" she cried.

"Zeus's shield!" I suddenly remembered. "Aegis. Thalia, the bracelet—it's got a code word!"

It was a desperate guess. Thank the gods—or thank blind luck—Thalia understood. She tapped the bracelet, but this time she yelled, "Aegis!"

Instantly the bracelet expanded, flattening into a wide bronze disk—a shield with intricate designs hammered around the rim. In the center, pressed into the metal like a death mask, was a face so hideous I would've run from it if I could've. I looked away, but the afterimage burned in my mind—snaky hair, glaring eyes, and a mouth with bared fangs.

Thalia thrust the shield toward the leucrota. The monster yelped like a puppy and retreated, freeing me from the weight of its hoof. Through the smoke, I watched the terrified leucrota run straight into the nearest drapes, which turned into glistening black tongues and engulfed the monster. The monster steamed. It began yelling, "Help!" in a dozen voices, probably the voices of its past victims, until finally it disintegrated in the dark oily folds.

I would've lain there stunned and horrified until the fiery ceiling collapsed on me, but Thalia grabbed my arm and yelled, "Hurry!"

We bolted for the front door. I was wondering how we'd open it, when the avalanche of fire poured down the staircase and caught us. The building exploded.

———

I can't remember how we got out. I can only assume that the shockwave blasted the front door open and pushed us outside.

The next thing I knew, I was sprawled in the traffic circle, coughing and gasping as a tower of fire roared into the evening sky. My throat burned. My eyes felt like they'd been splashed with acid. I looked for Thalia and instead found myself staring at the bronze face of Medusa. I screamed, somehow found the energy to stand, and ran. I didn't stop until I was cowering behind the statue of Robert E. Lee.

Yeah, I know. It sounds comical now. But it's a miracle I didn't have a heart attack or get hit by a car. Finally Thalia caught up to me, her spear back in Mace canister form, her shield reduced to a silver bracelet.

Together we stood and watched the mansion burn. Bricks crumbled. Black draperies burst into sheets of red fire. The roof collapsed and smoke billowed into the sky.

Thalia let loose a sob. A tear etched through the soot on her face.

"He sacrificed himself," she said. "Why did he save us?"

I hugged my knapsack. I felt the diary and bronze dagger inside—the only remnants of Halcyon Green's life.

My chest was tight, as if the leucrota was still standing on it. I'd criticized for Hal for being a coward, but in the end, he'd been braver than me. The gods had cursed him. He'd spent most of his life imprisoned with monsters. It would've been easy for him to let us die like all the other demigods before us. Yet he'd chosen to go out a hero.

I felt guilty that I couldn't save the old man. I wished I could've talked to him longer. What had he seen in my future that scared him so much?

Your choices will change the world, he'd warned.

I didn't like the sound of it.

The sound of sirens brought me to my senses.

Being runaway minors, Thalia and I had learned to distrust the police and anybody else with authority. The mortals would want to question us, maybe put us in juvie hall or foster care. We couldn't let that happen.

"Come on," I told Thalia.

We ran through the streets of Richmond until we found a small park. We cleaned up in the public restrooms as best we could. Then we lay low until full dark.

We didn't talk about what had happened. We wandered in a daze through neighborhoods and industrial areas. We had no plan, no glowing goat to follow anymore. We were bone tired, but neither of us felt like sleeping or stopping. I wanted to get as far as possible from that burning mansion.

It wasn't the first time we'd barely escaped with our lives, but we'd never succeeded at the expense of another demigod's life. I couldn't shake my grief.

Promise, Halcyon Green had written.

I promise, Hal, I thought. *I will learn from your mistakes. If the gods ever treat me that badly, I will fight back.*

Okay, I know that sounds like crazy talk. But I was feeling bitter and angry. If that makes the dudes up on Mount Olympus unhappy, tough. They can come down here and tell me to my face.

We stopped for a rest near an old warehouse. In the dim light of the moon, I could see a name painted on the side of the red brick building: RICHMOND IRON WORKS. Most of the windows were broken.

Thalia shivered. "We could head to our old camp," she suggested. "On the James River. We've got plenty of supplies down there."

I nodded apathetically. It would take at least a day to get there, but it was as good a plan as any.

I split my ham sandwich with Thalia. We ate in silence. The food tasted like cardboard. I'd just swallowed the last bite when I heard a faint metal *ping* from a nearby alley. My ears started tingling. We weren't alone.

"Someone's close by," I said. "Not a regular mortal."

Thalia tensed. "How can you be sure?"

I didn't have an answer, but I rose to my feet. I pulled out Hal's dagger, mostly for the glow of the Celestial bronze. Thalia grabbed her spear and summoned Aegis. This time I knew better than to look at the face of Medusa, but its presence still made my skin crawl. I didn't know if this shield was *the* aegis, or a replica made for heroes—but either way, it radiated power. I understood why Amaltheia had wanted Thalia to claim it.

We crept along the wall of the warehouse.

We turned into a dark alleyway that dead-ended at a loading dock piled with old scrap metal.

I pointed at the platform.

Thalia frowned. She whispered, "Are you sure?"

I nodded. "Something's down there. I sense it."

Just then there was a loud *CLANG*. A sheet of corrugated tin quivered on the dock. Something—*someone*—was underneath.

We crept toward the loading bay until we stood over the pile of metal. Thalia readied her spear. I gestured for her to hold back. I reached for the piece of corrugated metal and mouthed, *One, two, three!*

As soon as I lifted the sheet of tin, something flew at me—a blur of flannel and blond hair. A hammer hurtled straight at my face.

Things could've gone very wrong. Fortunately my reflexes were good from years of fighting.

I shouted, "Whoa!" and dodged the hammer, then grabbed the little girl's wrist. The hammer went skidding across the pavement.

The little girl struggled. She couldn't have been more than seven years old.

"No more monsters!" she screamed, kicking me in the legs. "Go away!"

"It's okay!" I tried my best to hold her, but it was like holding a wildcat. Thalia looked too stunned to move. She still had her spear and shield ready.

"Thalia," I said, "put your shield away! You're scaring her!"

Thalia unfroze. She touched the shield and it shrank back into a bracelet. She dropped her spear.

"Hey, little girl," she said, sounding more gentle than I'd ever heard. "It's all right. We're not going to hurt you. I'm Thalia. This is Luke."

"Monsters!" she wailed.

"No," I promised. The poor thing wasn't fighting as hard, but she was shivering like crazy, terrified of us. "But we know about monsters," I said. "We fight them too."

I held her, more to comfort than restrain now. Eventually she stopped kicking. She felt cold. Her ribs were bony under her flannel pajamas. I wondered how long this little girl had gone without eating. She was even younger than I had been when I ran away.

Despite her fear, she looked at me with large eyes. They were startlingly gray, beautiful and intelligent. A demigod—no doubt about it. I got the feeling she was powerful—or she would be, if she survived.

"You're like me?" she asked, still suspicious, but she sounded a little hopeful, too.

"Yeah," I promised. "We're . . ." I hesitated, not sure if she understood what she was, or if she'd ever heard the word *demigod*. I didn't want to scare her even worse. "Well, it's hard to explain, but we're monster fighters. Where's your family?"

The little girl's expression turned hard and angry. Her chin trembled. "My family hates me. They don't want me. I ran away."

My heart felt like it was cracking into pieces. She had such pain in her voice—familiar pain. I looked at Thalia, and we made a silent decision right there. We would take care of this kid. After what had happened with Halcyon Green . . . well, it seemed like fate. We'd watch one demigod die for us. Now we'd found this little girl. It was almost like a second chance.

Thalia knelt next to me. She put her hand on the little girl's shoulder. "What's your name, kiddo?"

"Annabeth."

I couldn't help smiling. I'd never heard that name before, but it was pretty, and it seemed to fit her. "Nice name," I told her. "I tell you what, Annabeth. You're pretty fierce. We could use a fighter like you."

Her eyes widened. "You could?"

"Oh, yeah," I said earnestly. Then a sudden thought struck me. I reached for Hal's dagger and pulled it from my belt. *It will protect its owner*, Hal had said. He had gotten it from the little girl he had saved. Now fate had given us the chance to save another little girl.

"How'd you like a real monster-slaying weapon?" I asked her. "This is Celestial bronze. Works a lot better than a hammer."

Annabeth took the dagger and studied it in awe. I know . . . she was seven years old at most. What was I thinking giving her a weapon? But she was a demigod. We have to defend ourselves. Hercules was only a baby when he strangled two snakes in his cradle. By the time I was nine, I'd fought for my life a dozen times. Annabeth could use a weapon.

"Knives are only for the bravest and quickest fighters," I told her. My voice caught as I remembered Hal Green, and how he'd died to save us. "They don't have the reach or power of a sword, but they're easy to conceal and they can find weak spots in your enemy's armor. It takes a clever warrior to use a knife. I have a feeling you're pretty clever."

Annabeth beamed at me, and for that instant, all my problems seemed to melt. I felt as if I'd done one thing right. I swore to myself I would never let this girl come to harm.

"I am clever!" she said.

Thalia laughed and tousled Annabeth's hair. Just like that—we had a new companion.

"We'd better get going, Annabeth," Thalia said. "We have a safe house on the James River. We'll get you some clothes and food."

Annabeth's smile wavered. For a moment, she got that wild look in her eyes again. "You're . . . you're not going to take me back to my family? Promise?"

I swallowed the lump out of my throat. Annabeth was so young, but she'd learned a hard lesson, just like Thalia and I had. Our parents had failed us. The gods were harsh and cruel and aloof. Demigods had only each other.

I put my hand on Annabeth's shoulder. "You're part of *our* family now. And I promise I'm not going to fail you like our families did us. Deal?"

"Deal!" she said happily, clutching her new dagger.

Thalia picked up her spear. She smiled at me with approval. "Now, come on. We can't stay put for long!"

———

So here I am on guard duty, writing in Halcyon Green's diary—*my* diary, now.

We're camping in the woods south of Richmond. Tomorrow, we'll press on to the James River and restock our supplies. After that . . . I don't know. I keep thinking about Hal Green's predictions. An ominous feeling weighs on my chest. There's something dark in my future. It may be a long way off, but it feels like a thunderstorm on the horizon, supercharging the air. I just hope I have the strength to take care of my friends.

Looking at Thalia and Annabeth asleep by the fire, I'm amazed how peaceful their faces are. If I'm going to be the "dad" of this bunch, I've got to be worthy of their trust. None of us has had good luck with our dads. I have to be better than that. I may be only fourteen, but that's no excuse. I have to keep my new family together.

I look toward the north. I imagine how long it would take to get to my mom's house in Westport, Connecticut, from here. I wonder what my mom is doing right now. She was in such a bad state of mind when I left. . . .

But I can't feel guilty about leaving her. I *had* to. If I ever meet my dad, we're going to have a conversation about that.

For now, I'll just have to survive day to day. I'll write in this diary as I have the chance, though I doubt anyone will ever read it.

Thalia is stirring. It's her turn on guard duty. Wow, my hand hurts. I haven't written this much in forever. I'd better sleep, and hope for no dreams.

Luke Castellan—signing off for now.

DANGERS OF HAL'S HOUSE

GREEKS AND ROMANS

*Let your knowledge of Greek and Roman gods
guide you to a secret message!*

The chart below lists the name of Greek and Roman gods. Your challenge: Match the proper Greek and Roman names to the description in the chart on the opposite page.

When you're done, replace the letters assigned to each Greek god with his or her Roman counterpart's assigned number to reveal a hidden message!

GREEK GODS	**ROMAN GODS**
1. Hephaestus	A. Jupiter
2. Kronos	B. Faunus
3. Aphrodite	C. Vulcan
4. Poseidon	D. Juno
5. Hermes	E. Ceres
6. Zeus	F. Bacchus
7. Demeter	G. Venus
8. Ares	H. Apollo
9. Hera	I. Mercury
10. Gaea	J. Arcus
11. Pan	K. Janus
12. Dionysus	L. Neptune
13. Hades	M. Terra
14. Apollo	N. Mars
15. Iris	O. Pluto
16. Hecate	P. Trivia

Where do Luke, Thalia, and Annabeth find a home?

$\overline{}\ \overline{}\ \overline{}\ \overline{}$ $\overline{}\ \overline{}\ \overline{}\ \overline{}$ - $\overline{}\ \overline{}\ \overline{}\ \overline{}\ \overline{}$

1 6 10 16   14 6 4 12   11 4 13 13 9

Greek Gods	Characteristics	Roman Gods
	The patroness of love and beauty	
	God of music, prophecy, medicine, poetry (loves haikus!), and intellectual inquiry	
	A love of violence makes this god of war a fearsome avenger	
	Zeus's sister, she is credited for teaching man to farm	
	The god of wine who loves parties, but is kind of a grump. In Roman form, he becomes more disciplined and warlike.	
	Born from chaos, this "Mother Earth" is anything but maternal to the Olympians!	
	One of the "big three," he's the god of wealth and the dead, and the king of the underworld	
	A daughter of the Titans, this goddess is often seen as the patroness of magic	
	God of fire and patron of craftsmen; his forges were associated with earthquakes and volcanoes	
	As Zeus's wife, she's the queen of the gods, and a powerful goddess in her own right	
	He travels all over as the god of roads, speed, messengers, commerce, travel, thieves, merchants, and mail deliverers	
	She loves rainbows and keeps busy relaying messages to and from gods, demigods, and even Titans	
	These deities both represent the passage of time—personified by age in Greece, by gateways and beginnings/endings in Rome	
	The only god on this list with horns (he's a satyr), he's a patron of the Wild and protector of flocks and herds	
	God of the sea, earthquakes, fresh water, and horses—also, Percy Jackson's dad!	
	Powerful and proud, he's the king of the gods and associated with law, justice, and morality	

ANSWER KEY

GREEK GODS	CHARACTERISTICS	ROMAN GODS
(3) Aphrodite	The patroness of love and beauty	(G) Venus
(14) Apollo	God of music, prophecy, medicine, poetry (loves haikus!), and intellectual inquiry	(H) Apollo
(8) Ares	A love of violence makes this god of war a fearsome avenger	(N) Mars
(7) Demeter	Zeus's sister, she is credited for teaching man to farm	(E) Ceres
(12) Dionysus	The god of wine who loves parties, but is kind of a grump. In Roman form, he becomes more disciplined and warlike.	(F) Bacchus
(10) Gaea	Born from chaos, this "Mother Earth" is anything but maternal to the Olympians!	(M) Terra
(13) Hades	One of the "big three," he's the god of wealth and the dead, and the king of the underworld	(O) Pluto
(16) Hecate	A daughter of the Titans, this goddess is often seen as the patroness of magic	(P) Trivia
(1) Hephaestus	God of fire and patron of craftsmen; his forges were associated with earthquakes and volcanoes	(C) Vulcan
(9) Hera	As Zeus's wife, she's the queen of the gods, and a powerful goddess in her own right	(D) Juno
(5) Hermes	He travels all over as the god of roads, speed, messengers, commerce, travel, thieves, merchants, and mail deliverers	(I) Mercury
(15) Iris	She loves rainbows and keeps busy relaying messages to and from gods, demigods, and even Titans	(J) Arcus
(2) Kronos	These deities both represent the passage of time—personified by age in Greece, by gateways and beginnings/endings in Rome	(K) Janus
(11) Pan	The only god on this list with horns (he's a satyr), he's a patron of the Wild and protector of flocks and herds	(B) Faunus
(4) Poseidon	God of the sea, earthquakes, fresh water, and horses—also, Percy Jackson's dad!	(L) Neptune
(6) Zeus	Powerful and proud, he's the king of the gods and associated with law, justice, and morality	(A) Jupiter

CODED MESSAGE ANSWER

Camp Half-Blood

PERCY JACKSON
AND THE
STAFF OF HERMES

ANNABETH AND I WERE RELAXING on the Great Lawn in Central Park when she ambushed me with a question.

"You forgot, didn't you?"

I went into red-alert mode. It's easy to panic when you're a new boyfriend. Sure, I'd fought monsters with Annabeth for years. Together we'd faced the wrath of the gods. We'd battled Titans and calmly faced death a dozen times. But now that we were dating, one frown from her and I freaked. What had I done wrong?

I mentally reviewed the picnic list: Comfy blanket? Check. Annabeth's favorite pizza with extra olives? Check. Chocolate toffee from La Maison du Chocolat? Check. Chilled sparkling water with twist of lemon? Check. Weapons in case of sudden Greek mythological apocalypse? Check.

So what had I forgotten?

I was tempted (briefly) to bluff my way through. Two things stopped me. First, I didn't want to lie to Annabeth. Second, she was too smart. She'd see right through me.

So I did what I do best. I stared at her blankly and acted dumb.

Annabeth rolled her eyes. "Percy, today is September eighteenth. What happened exactly one month ago?"

"It was my birthday," I said.

That was true: August eighteenth. But judging from Annabeth's expression, that wasn't the answer she'd been hoping for.

It didn't help my concentration that Annabeth looked so good today. She was wearing her regular orange camp T-shirt and shorts, but her tan arms and legs seemed to glow in the sunlight. Her blond hair swept over her shoulders. Around her neck hung a leather cord with colorful beads from our demigod training camp—Camp Half-Blood. Her storm-gray eyes were as dazzling as ever. I just wished that their fierce look wasn't directed at me.

I tried to think. One month ago we'd defeated the Titan Kronos. Was that what she meant? Then Annabeth set my priorities straight.

"Our first kiss, Seaweed Brain," she said. "It's our one-month anniversary."

"Well . . . yeah!" I thought: *Do people celebrate stuff like that? I have to remember birthdays, holidays,* and *all anniversaries?*

I tried for a smile. "That's why we're having this great picnic, right?"

She tucked her legs underneath her. "Percy . . . I love the picnic. Really. But you promised to take me out for a special dinner tonight. Remember? It's not that I *expect* it, but you said you had something planned. So . . . ?"

I could hear hopefulness in her voice, but also doubt. She was waiting for me to admit the obvious: I'd forgotten. I was toast. I was boyfriend roadkill.

Just because I forgot, you shouldn't take that as a sign I didn't care about Annabeth. Seriously, the last month with her had been awesome. I was the luckiest demigod ever. But a special dinner . . . when had I mentioned that? Maybe I'd said it after Annabeth kissed me, which had sort of sent me into a fog. Maybe a Greek god had disguised himself as me and made her that promise as a prank. Or maybe I was just a rotten boyfriend.

Time to fess up. I cleared my throat. "Well—"

A sudden streak of light made me blink, as if someone had flashed a mirror in my face. I looked around and I saw a brown delivery truck parked in the middle of the Great Lawn where no cars were allowed. Lettered on the side were the words:

HERNIAS ARE US

Wait . . . sorry. I'm dyslexic. I squinted and decided it probably read:

HERMES EXPRESS

"Oh, good," I muttered. "We've got mail."

"What?" Annabeth asked.

I pointed at the truck. The driver was climbing out. He wore a brown uniform shirt and knee-length shorts along with stylish black socks and cleats. His curly salt-and-pepper hair stuck out around the edges of his brown cap. He looked like a guy in his mid-thirties, but I knew from experience he was actually in his mid-five-thousands.

Hermes. Messenger of the gods. Personal friend, dispenser of heroic quests, and frequent cause of migraine headaches.

He looked upset. He kept patting his pockets and wringing his hands. Either he'd lost something important or he'd had too many espressos at the Mount Olympus Starbucks. Finally he spotted me and beckoned, *Get over here!*

That could've meant several things. If he was delivering a message in person from the gods, it was bad news. If he wanted something from me, it was also bad news. But seeing as he'd just saved me from explaining myself to Annabeth, I was too relieved to care.

"Bummer." I tried to sound regretful, as if my rump hadn't just been pulled from the barbecue. "We'd better see what he wants."

———

How do you greet a god? If there's an etiquette guide for that, I haven't read it. I'm never sure if I'm supposed to shake hands, kneel, or bow and shout, "We're not worthy!"

I knew Hermes better than most of the Olympians. Over the years, he'd helped me out several times. Unfortunately last summer I'd also fought his demigod son Luke, who'd been corrupted by the Titan Kronos, in a mortal combat smack-down for the fate of the world. Luke's death hadn't been entirely my fault, but it still put a damper on my relationship with Hermes.

I decided to start simple. "Hi."

Hermes scanned the park as if he was afraid of being watched. I'm not sure why he bothered. Gods are usually invisible to mortals. Nobody else on the Great Lawn was paying any attention to the delivery van.

Hermes glanced at Annabeth, then back at me. "I didn't know the girl would be here. She'll have to swear to keep her mouth shut."

Annabeth crossed her arms. "The *girl* can hear you. And before I swear to anything, maybe you'd better tell us what's wrong."

I don't think I've ever seen a god look so jittery. Hermes tucked a curl of gray hair behind his ear. He patted his pockets again. His hands didn't seem to know what to do.

He leaned in and lowered his voice. "I'm mean it, girl. If word gets back to Athena, she'll never stop teasing me. She already thinks she's so much cleverer than I am."

"She is," Annabeth said. Of course, she's prejudiced. Athena is her mom.

Hermes glared at her. "Promise. Before I explain the problem, both of you must promise to keep silent."

Suddenly it dawned on me. "Where's your staff?"

Hermes's eye twitched. He looked like he was about to cry.

"Oh, gods," Annabeth said. "You *lost* your staff?"

"I didn't lose it!" Hermes snapped. "It was stolen. And I wasn't asking for *your* help, girl!"

"Fine," she said. "Solve your own problem. Come on, Percy. Let's get out of here."

Hermes snarled. I realized I might have to break up a fight between an immortal god and my girlfriend, and I didn't want to be on either side of that.

A little background: Annabeth used to adventure with Hermes's son Luke. Over time, Annabeth developed a crush on Luke. As Annabeth got older, Luke developed feelings for her, too. Luke turned evil. Hermes blamed Annabeth for not preventing Luke from turning evil. Annabeth blamed Hermes for being a rotten dad and giving Luke the capacity to become evil in the first place. Luke died in war. Hermes and Annabeth blamed each other.

Confused? Welcome to my world.

Anyway, I figured things would go badly if these two went nuclear, so I risked stepping between them. "Annabeth, tell you what. This sounds important. Let me hear him out, and I'll meet you back at the picnic blanket, okay?"

I gave her a smile that I hoped conveyed something like: *Hey, you know I'm on your side. Gods are such jerks! But what can you do?*

Probably my expression actually conveyed: *It's not my fault! Please do not kill me!*

Before she could protest or cause me bodily harm, I grabbed Hermes's arm. "Let's step into your office."

———•———

Hermes and I sat in the back of the delivery truck on a couple of boxes labeled TOXIC SERPENTS. THIS END UP. Maybe that wasn't the best place to sit, but it was better than some of his other deliveries, which were labeled EXPLOSIVES, DO NOT SIT ON, and DRAKON EGGS, DO NOT STORE NEAR EXPLOSIVES.

"So what happened?" I asked him.

Hermes slumped on his delivery boxes. He stared at his empty hands. "I only left them alone for a minute."

"Them . . ." I said. "Oh, George and Martha?"

Hermes nodded dejectedly.

George and Martha were the two snakes that wrapped around his caduceus—his staff of power. You've probably seen pictures of the caduceus at hospitals, since it's often used as a symbol for doctors. (Annabeth would argue and say that whole thing is a misconception. It's supposed to be the staff of Asclepius the medicine god, blah, blah, blah. But whatever.)

I was kind of fond of George and Martha. I got the feeling Hermes was too, even though he was constantly arguing with them.

"I made a stupid mistake," he muttered. "I was late with a delivery. I stopped at Rockefeller Center and was delivering a box of doormats to Janus—"

"Janus," I said. "The two-faced guy, god of doorways."

"Yes, yes. He works there. Network television."

"Say what?" The last time I'd met Janus he'd been in a deadly magical labyrinth, and the experience hadn't been pleasant.

Hermes rolled his eyes. "Surely you've *seen* network TV lately. It's clear they don't know whether they're coming or going. That's because Janus is in charge of programming. He loves ordering new shows and canceling them after two episodes. God of beginnings and endings, after all. Anyway, I was bringing him some magic doormats, and I was double-parked—"

"You have to worry about double-parking?"

"Will you let me tell the story?"

"Sorry."

"So I left my caduceus on the dashboard and ran inside with the box. Then I realized I needed to have Janus sign for the delivery, so I ran back to the truck—"

"And the caduceus was gone."

Hermes nodded. "If that ugly brute has harmed my snakes, I swear by the Styx—"

"Hold on. You know who took the staff?"

Hermes snorted. "Of course. I checked the security cameras

in the area. I talked with the wind nymphs. The thief was clearly Cacus."

"Cacus." I'd had years of practice looking dumb when people threw out Greek names I didn't know. It's a skill of mine. Annabeth keeps telling me to read a book of Greek myths, but I don't see the need. It's easier just to have folks explain stuff.

"Good old Cacus," I said. "I should probably know who that is—"

"Oh, he's a giant," Hermes said dismissively. "A *small* giant, not one of the big ones."

"A small giant."

"Yes. Maybe ten feet tall."

"Tiny, then," I agreed.

"He's a well-known thief. Stole Apollo's cattle once."

"I thought *you* stole Apollo's cattle."

"Well, yes. But I did it first, and with much more style. At any rate, Cacus is always stealing things from the gods. Very annoying. He used to hide out in a cave on Capitoline Hill, where Rome was founded. Nowadays, he's in Manhattan. Underground somewhere, I'm sure."

I took a deep breath. I saw where this was going. "Now you're going to explain to me why you, a superpowerful god, can't just go get your staff back yourself, and why you need me, a sixteen-year-old kid, to do it for you."

Hermes tilted his head. "Percy, that almost sounded like sarcasm. You know very well the gods can't go around busting heads and ripping up mortal cities looking for our lost items. If we did that, New York would be destroyed every time Aphrodite lost her hairbrush, and believe me, that happens *a lot*. We need heroes for that sort of errand."

"Uh-huh. And if you went looking for the staff yourself, it might be a little embarrassing."

Hermes pursed his lips. "All right. Yes. The other gods would certainly take notice. Me, the god of thieves, being stolen from. And my *caduceus*, no less, symbol of my power! I'd be ridiculed for centuries. The idea is too horrible. I need this resolved quickly and quietly before I become the laughingstock of Olympus."

"So . . . you want us find this giant, get back your caduceus, and return it to you. Quietly."

Hermes smiled. "What a fine offer! Thank you. And I'll need it before five o'clock this evening so I can finish my deliveries. The caduceus serves as my signature pad, my GPS, my phone, my parking permit, my iPod Shuffle—really, I can't do a thing without it."

"By five." I didn't have a watch, but I was pretty sure it was at least one o'clock already. "Can you be more specific about where Cacus is?"

Hermes shrugged. "I'm sure you can figure that out. And just a warning: Cacus breathes fire."

"Naturally," I said.

"And do be mindful of the caduceus. The tip can turn people to stone. I had to do that once with this horrible tattletale named Battus . . . but I'm sure you'll be careful. And of course you'll keep this as our little secret."

He smiled winningly. Maybe I was imagining that he'd just threatened to petrify me if I told anyone about the theft.

I swallowed the sawdust taste out of my mouth. "Of course."

"You'll do it, then?"

An idea occurred to me. Yes—I do get ideas occasionally.

"How about we trade favors?" I suggested. "I help you with your embarrassing situation; you help me with mine."

Hermes raised an eyebrow. "What did you have in mind?"

"You're the god of travel, right?"

"Of course."

I told him what I wanted for my reward.

————

I was in better spirits when I rejoined Annabeth. I'd made arrangements to meet Hermes at Rockefeller Center no later than five, and his delivery truck had disappeared in a flash of light. Annabeth waited by our picnic site with her arms folded indignantly.

"Well?" she demanded.

"Good news." I told her what we had to do.

She didn't slap me, but she looked like she wanted to. "Why is tracking down a fire-breathing giant good news? And why do I want to help out Hermes?"

"He's not so bad," I said. "Besides, two innocent snakes are in trouble. George and Martha must be terrified—"

"Is this an elaborate joke?" she asked. "Tell me you planned this with Hermes, and we're actually going to a surprise party for our anniversary."

"Um . . . Well, no. But afterward, I promise—"

Annabeth raised her hand. "You're cute and you're sweet, Percy. But please—no more promises. Let's just find this giant."

She stowed our blanket in her backpack and put away the food. Sad . . . since I'd barely tasted any of the pizza. The only thing she kept out was her shield.

Like a lot of magic items, it was designed to morph into a smaller item for easy carrying. The shield shrinks to plate size, which is what we'd been using it for. Great for cheese and crackers.

Annabeth brushed off the crumbs and tossed the plate into the air. It expanded as it spun. When it landed in the grass it was a full-sized bronze shield, its highly polished surface reflecting the sky.

The shield had come in handy during our war with the Titans, but I wasn't sure how it could help us now.

"That thing only shows aerial images, right?" I asked. "Cacus is supposed to be underground."

Annabeth shrugged. "Worth a try. Shield, I want to see Cacus."

Light rippled across the bronze surface.

Instead of a reflection, we were looking down at a landscape of dilapidated warehouses and crumbling roads. A rusty water tower rose above the urban blight.

Annabeth snorted. "This stupid shield has a sense of humor."

"What do you mean?" I asked.

"That's *Secaucus*, New Jersey. Read the sign on the water tower." She rapped her knuckles on the bronze surface. "Okay, very funny, shield. Now I want to see—I mean, show me the location of the fire-breathing giant Cacus."

The image changed.

This time I saw a familiar part of Manhattan: renovated warehouses, brick-paved streets, a glass hotel, and an elevated train track that had been turned into a park with trees and wildflowers. I remembered my mom and stepdad taking me there a few years ago when it first opened.

"That's the High Line park," I said. "In the Meatpacking District."

"Yeah," Annabeth agreed. "But where's the giant?"

She frowned in concentration. The shield zoomed in on an intersection blocked off with orange barricades and detour signs.

Construction equipment sat idle in the shadow of the High Line. Chiseled in the street was big square hole, cordoned off with yellow police tape. Steam billowed from the pit.

I scratched my head. "Why would the police seal off a hole in the street?"

"I remember this," Annabeth said. "It was on the news yesterday."

"I don't watch the news."

"A construction worker got hurt. Some freak accident way below the surface. They were digging a new service tunnel or something, and a fire broke out."

"A fire," I said. "As in, maybe a fire-breathing giant?"

"That would make sense," she agreed. "The mortals wouldn't understand what was happening. The Mist would obscure what they really saw. They'd think the giant was just like—I don't know—a gas explosion or something."

"So let's catch a cab."

Annabeth gazed wistfully across the Great Lawn. "First sunny day in weeks, and my boyfriend wants to take me to a dangerous cave to fight a fire-breathing giant."

"You're awesome," I said.

"I know," Annabeth said. "You'd better have something good planned for dinner."

The cab dropped us off on West 15th. The streets were bustling with a mix of sidewalk vendors, workers, shoppers, and tourists. Why a place called the Meatpacking District was suddenly a hot area to hang out, I wasn't sure. But that's the cool thing about New York. It's always changing. Apparently even monsters wanted to stay here.

We made our way to the construction site. Two police officers stood at the intersection, but they didn't pay us any attention as we turned up the sidewalk and then doubled back, ducking behind the barricades.

The hole in the street was about the size of a garage door. Pipe scaffolding hung over it with a sort of winch system, and metal climbing rungs had been fastened into the side of the pit, leading down.

"Ideas?" I asked Annabeth.

I figured I'd ask. Being the daughter of the goddess of wisdom and strategy, Annabeth likes making plans.

"We climb down," she said. "We find the giant. We get the caduceus."

"Wow," I said. "Both wise and strategic."

"Shut up."

We climbed over the barricade, ducked under the police tape, and crept toward the hole. I kept a wary eye on the police, but they didn't turn around. Sneaking into a dangerous steaming pit in the middle of a New York intersection proved disturbingly easy.

We descended. And descended.

The rungs seemed to go down forever. The square of daylight above us got smaller and smaller until it was the size of a postage stamp. I couldn't hear the city traffic anymore, just the echo of trickling water. Every twenty feet or so, a dim light flickered next to the ladder, but the descent was still gloomy and creepy.

I was vaguely aware that the tunnel was opening up behind me into a much larger space, but I stayed focused on the ladder, trying not to step on Annabeth's hands as she climbed below me. I didn't realize we'd reached the bottom until I heard Annabeth's feet splash.

"Holy Hephaestus," she said. "Percy, look."

I dropped next to her in a shallow puddle of muck. I turned and found that we were standing in a factory-sized cavern. Our tunnel emptied into it like a narrow chimney. The rock walls bristled with old cables, pipe, and lines of brickwork—maybe the foundations of old buildings. Busted water pipes, possibly old sewer lines, sent a steady drizzle of water down the walls, turning the floor muddy. I didn't want to know what was in that water.

There wasn't much light, but the cavern looked like a cross between a construction zone and a flea market. Scattered around the cave were crates, toolboxes, pallets of timber, and stacks of steel pipe. There was even a bulldozer half-sunken in the mud.

Even stranger: several old cars had somehow been brought from the surface, each filled with suitcases and mounds of purses. Racks of clothing had been carelessly tossed around like somebody had cleaned out a department store. Worst of all, hanging from meat hooks on a stainless steel scaffold was a row of cow carcasses—skinned, gutted, and ready for butchering. Judging from the smell and the flies, they weren't very fresh. It was almost enough to make me turn vegetarian, except for the pesky fact that I loved cheeseburgers.

No sign of a giant. I hoped he wasn't home. Then Annabeth pointed to the far end of the cave. "Maybe down there."

Leading into the darkness was a twenty-foot-diameter tunnel, perfectly round, as if made by a huge snake. Oh . . . bad thought.

I didn't like the idea of walking to the other side of the cave, especially through that flea market of heavy machinery and cow carcasses.

"How did all this stuff get down here?" I felt the need to whisper, but my voice echoed anyway.

Annabeth scanned the scene. She obviously didn't like what she saw. "They must've lowered the bulldozer in pieces and assembled it down here," she decided. "I think that's how they dug the subway system a long time ago."

"What about the other junk?" I asked. "The cars and, um, meat products?"

She furrowed her eyebrows. "Some of it looks like street vendor merchandise. Those purses and coats . . . the giant must've brought them down here for some reason." She gestured toward the bulldozer. "That thing looks like it's been through combat."

As my eyes adjusted to the gloom, I saw what she meant. The machine's caterpillar treads were busted. The driver's seat was charred to a crisp. In the front of the rig, the big shovel blade was dented as if it had run into something . . . or been punched.

The silence was eerie. Looking up at the tiny speck of daylight above us, I got vertigo. How could a cave this big exist under Manhattan without the city block collapsing, or the Hudson River flooding in? We had to be hundreds of feet below sea level.

What really disturbed me was that tunnel on the far side of the cave.

I'm not saying I can smell monsters the way my friend Grover the satyr can. But suddenly I understood why he hated being underground. It felt oppressive and dangerous. Demigods didn't belong here. Something was waiting down that tunnel.

I glanced at Annabeth, hoping she had a great idea—like running away. Instead, she started toward the bulldozer.

We'd just reached the middle of the cave when a groan echoed from the far tunnel. We ducked behind the bulldozer just as the giant appeared from the darkness, stretching his massive arms.

"Breakfast," he rumbled.

I could see him clearly now, and I wished I couldn't.

How ugly was he? Let's put it this way: Secaucus, New Jersey, was a lot nicer-looking than Cacus the giant, and that's not a compliment to anybody.

As Hermes had said, the giant was about ten feet tall, which made him small compared to some other giants I'd seen. But Cacus made up for it by being bright and gaudy. He had curly orange hair, pale skin, and orange freckles. His face was smeared upward with a permanent pout, upturned nose, wide eyes, and arched eyebrows, so he appeared both startled and unhappy. He wore a red velour housecoat with matching slippers. The housecoat was open, revealing silky Valentine-patterned boxer shorts and luxurious chest hair of a red/pink/orange color not found in nature.

Annabeth made a small gagging sound. "It's the ginger giant."

Unfortunately, the giant had extremely good hearing. He frowned and scanned the cavern, zeroing in on our hiding place.

"Who's there?" he bellowed. "You—behind the bulldozer."

Annabeth and I looked at each other. She mouthed, *Oops.*

"Come on!" the giant said. "I don't appreciate sneaking about! Show yourself."

That sounded like a really terrible idea. Then again, we were pretty much busted anyway. Maybe the giant would listen to reason, despite the fact that he wore Valentine boxer shorts.

I took out my ballpoint pen and uncapped it. My bronze sword

Riptide sprang to life. Annabeth pulled out her shield and dagger. None of our weapons looked very intimidating against a dude that big, but together we stepped into the open.

The giant grinned. "Well! Demigods, are you? I call for breakfast, and you two appear? That's quite accommodating."

"We're not breakfast," Annabeth said.

"No?" The giant stretched lazily. Twin wisps of smoke escaped his nostrils. "I imagine you'd taste wonderful with tortillas, salsa, and eggs. *Huevos semidiós.* Just thinking about it makes me hungry!"

He sauntered over to the row of fly-specked cow carcasses.

My stomach twisted. I muttered, "Oh, he's not really gonna—"

Cacus snatched one of the carcasses off a hook. He blew fire over it—a red-hot torrent of flame that cooked the meat in seconds but didn't seem to hurt the giant's hands at all. Once the cow was crispy and sizzling, Cacus unhinged his jaw, opening his mouth impossibly wide, and downed the carcass in three massive bites, bones and all.

"Yep," Annabeth said weakly. "He really did it."

The giant belched. He wiped his steaming greasy hands on his robe and grinned at us. "So, if you're not breakfast, you must be customers. What can I interest you in?"

He sounded relaxed and friendly, like he was happy to talk with us. Between that and the red velour housecoat, he almost didn't seem dangerous. Except of course that he was ten feet tall, blew fire, and ate cows in three bites.

I stepped forward. Call me old-fashioned, but I wanted to keep his focus on me and not Annabeth. I think it's polite for a guy to protect his girlfriend from instant incineration.

"Um, yeah," I said. "We might be customers. What do you sell?"

Cacus laughed. "What do I sell? Everything, demigod! At bargain basement prices, and you can't find a basement lower than this!" He gestured around the cavern. "I've got designer handbags, Italian suits, um . . . some construction equipment, apparently, and if you're in the market for a Rolex . . ."

He opened his robe. Pinned to the inside was a glittering array of gold and silver watches.

Annabeth snapped her fingers. "Fakes! I *knew* I'd seen that stuff before. You got all this from street merchants, didn't you? They're designer knockoffs."

The giant looked offended. "Not just *any* knockoffs, young lady. I steal only the best! I'm a son of Hephaestus. I know quality fakes when I see them."

I frowned. "A son of Hephaestus? Then shouldn't you be *making* things rather than stealing them?"

Cacus snorted. "Too much work! Oh, sometimes if I find a high-quality item I'll make my own copies. But mostly it's easier to steal things. I started with cattle thieving, you know, back in the old days. Love cattle! That's why I settled in the Meatpacking District. Then I discovered they have more than meat here!"

He grinned as if this was an amazing discovery. "Street vendors, high-end boutiques—this is a wonderful city, even better than Ancient Rome! And the workers were very nice to make me this cave."

"Before you ran them off," Annabeth said, "and almost killed them."

Cacus stifled a yawn. "Are you sure you're not breakfast? Because you're beginning to bore me. If you don't want to buy something, I'll go get the salsa and tortillas—"

"We were looking for something special," I interrupted. "Something real. And magic. But I guess you don't have anything like that."

"Ha!" Cacus clapped his hands. "A high-end shopper. If I haven't got what you need in stock, I can steal it, for the right price, of course."

"Hermes's staff," I said. "The caduceus."

The giant's face turned as red as his hair. His eyes narrowed. "I see. I should've known Hermes would send someone. Who are you two? Children of the thief god?"

Annabeth raised her knife. "Did he just call me Hermes's kid? I'm going stab him in the—"

"I'm Percy Jackson, son of Poseidon," I told the giant. I put out my arm to hold Annabeth back. "This is Annabeth Chase, daughter of Athena. We help out the gods sometimes with little stuff, like—oh, killing Titans, saving Mount Olympus, things like that. Perhaps you've heard stories. So about that caduceus . . . it would be easier just to hand it over before things get unpleasant."

I looked him in the eyes and hoped my threat would work. I know it seems ridiculous, a sixteen-year-old trying to stare down a fire-breathing giant. But I *had* battled some pretty serious monsters before. Plus, I'd bathed in the River Styx, which made me immune to most physical attacks. That should be worth a little street cred, right? Maybe Cacus had heard of me. Maybe he would tremble and whimper, *Oh, Mr. Jackson. I'm so sorry! I didn't realize!*

Instead he threw back his head and laughed. "Oh, I see! That was supposed to scare me! But alas, the only demigod who ever defeated me was Hercules himself."

I turned to Annabeth and shook my head in exasperation. "Always Hercules. What is it with Hercules?"

Annabeth shrugged. "He had a great publicist."

The giant kept boasting. "For centuries, I was the terror of Italy! I stole many cows—more than any other giant. Mothers used to scare their children with my name. They would say, 'Mind your manners, child, or Cacus will come and steal your cows!'"

"Horrifying," Annabeth said.

The giant grinned. "I know! Right? So you may as well give

up, demigods. You'll never get the caduceus. I have plans for that!"

He raised his hand and the staff of Hermes appeared in his grip. I'd seen it many times before, but it still sent a shiver down my back. Godly items just radiate power. The staff was smooth white wood about three feet long, topped with a silver sphere and dove's wings that fluttered nervously. Intertwined around the staff were two live, very agitated serpents.

Percy! A reptilian voice spoke in my mind. *Thank the gods!*

Another snaky voice, deeper and grumpier, said, *Yes, I haven't been fed in hours.*

"Martha, George," I said. "Are you guys all right?"

Better if I got some food, George complained. *There are some nice rats down here. Could you catch us some?*

George, stop! Martha chided. *We have bigger problems. This giant wants to keep us!*

Cacus looked back and forth from me to the snakes. "Wait . . . You can speak with the snakes, Percy Jackson? That's excellent! Tell them they'd better start cooperating. I'm their new master, and they'll only get fed when they start taking orders."

The nerve! Martha shrieked. *You tell that ginger jerk—*

"Hold on," Annabeth interrupted. "Cacus, the snakes will never obey you. They only work for Hermes. Since you can't use the staff, it doesn't do you any good. Just give it back and we'll pretend this never happened."

"Great idea," I said.

The giant snarled. "Oh, I'll figure out the staff's powers, girl. I'll *make* the snakes cooperate!"

Cacus shook the caduceus. George and Martha wriggled and hissed, but they seemed stuck to the staff. I knew the caduceus could turn into all sorts of helpful things—a sword, a cell phone, a price scanner for easy comparison-shopping. And once George had mentioned something disturbing about "laser mode." I really didn't want Cacus figuring out that feature.

Finally the giant growled in frustration. He slammed the staff against the nearest cow carcass and instantly the meat turned to stone. A wave of petrifaction spread from carcass to carcass until the rack became so heavy it collapsed. Half a dozen granite cows broke to pieces.

"Now, *that's* interesting!" Cacus beamed.

"Uh-oh." Annabeth took a step back.

The giant swung the staff in our direction. "Yes! Soon I will master this thing and be as powerful as Hermes. I'll be able to go anywhere! I'll steal anything I want, make high-quality knock-offs, and sell them around the world. I will be the lord of traveling salesmen!"

"That," I said, "is truly evil."

"Ha-ha!" Cacus raised the caduceus in triumph. "I had my doubts, but now I'm convinced. Stealing this staff was an excellent idea! Now let's see how I can kill you with it."

"Wait!" Annabeth said. "You mean it wasn't your idea to steal the staff?"

"Kill them!" Cacus ordered the snakes. He pointed the caduceus at us, but the silver tip only spewed slips of paper. Annabeth picked up one and read it.

"You're trying to kill us with Groupons," she announced. "'Eighty-five percent off piano lessons.'"

"Gah!" Cacus glared at the snakes and breathed a fiery warning shot over their heads. "Obey me!"

George and Martha squirmed in alarm.

Stop that! Martha cried.

We're cold-blooded! George protested. *Fire is not good!*

"Hey, Cacus!" I shouted, trying to get back his attention. "Answer our question. Who told you to steal the staff?"

The giant sneered. "Foolish demigod. When you defeated Kronos, did you think you eliminated *all* the enemies of the gods? You only delayed the fall of Olympus for a little while longer. Without the staff, Hermes will be unable to carry messages. Olympian communication lines will be disrupted, and that's only the first bit of chaos my friends have planned."

"Your friends?" Annabeth asked.

Cacus waved off the question. "Doesn't matter. You won't live that long, and I'm only in it for the money. With this staff, I'll make millions! Maybe even thousands! Now hold still. Perhaps I can get a good price on two demigod statues."

I wasn't fond of threats like that. I'd had enough of them a few years ago when I fought Medusa. I wasn't anxious to fight this guy, but I also knew I couldn't leave George and Martha at his mercy. Besides, the world had enough traveling salesmen. Nobody deserved to answer their door and find a fire-breathing giant with a magic staff and a collection of knockoff Rolexes.

I looked at Annabeth. "Time to fight?"

She gave me a sweet smile. "Smartest thing you've said all morning."

———

You're probably thinking: Wait, you just charged in without a plan?

But Annabeth and I had been fighting together for years. We knew each other's abilities. We could anticipate each other's moves. I might have felt awkward and nervous about being her boyfriend, but fighting with her? That came naturally.

Hmm . . . that sounded wrong. Oh, well.

Annabeth veered to the giant's left. I charged him head-on. I was still out of sword-reach when Cacus unhinged his jaw and blew fire.

My next startling discovery: flaming breath is hot.

I managed to leap to one side, but I could feel my arms starting to warm up and my clothes igniting. I rolled through the mud to douse the flames and knocked over a rack of women's coats.

The giant roared. "Look what you've done! Those are genuine fake Prada!"

Annabeth used the distraction to strike. She lunged at Cacus from behind and stabbed him in the back of the knee—usually a nice soft spot on monsters. She leaped away as Cacus swung the caduceus, barely missing her. The silver tip slammed into the bulldozer and the entire machine turned to stone.

"I'll kill you!" Cacus stumbled, golden ichor pouring from his wounded leg.

He blew fire at Annabeth, but she dodged the blast. I lunged with Riptide and slashed my blade across the giant's other leg.

You'd think that would be enough, right? But no.

Cacus bellowed in pain. He turned with surprising speed, smacking me with the back of his hand. I went flying and crashed into a pile of broken stone cows. My vision blurred. Annabeth yelled, "Percy!" but her voice sounded as though it were underwater.

Move! Martha's voice spoke in my mind. *He's about to strike!*

Roll left! George said, which was one of the more helpful suggestions he'd ever made. I rolled to the left as the caduceus smashed into the pile of stone where I'd been lying.

I heard a *CLANG!* And the giant screamed, "Gah!"

I staggered to my feet. Annabeth had just smacked her shield across the giant's backside. Being an expert at school expulsion, I'd gotten kicked out of several military academies where they still believed paddling was good for the soul. I had a fair idea how it felt to get spanked with a large flat surface, and my rump clenched in sympathy.

Cacus staggered, but before Annabeth could discipline him again, he turned and snatched the shield from her. He crumpled the Celestial bronze like paper and tossed it over his shoulder.

So much for that magic item.

"Enough!" Cacus leveled the staff at Annabeth.

I was still dizzy. My spine felt like it had been treated to a night at Crusty's Water Bed Palace, but I stumbled forward, determined to help Annabeth. Before I could get there, the caduceus changed form. It became a cell phone and rang to the tune of "Macarena." George and Martha, now the size of earthworms, curled around the screen.

Good one, George said.

We danced to this at our wedding, Martha said. *Remember, dear?*

"Stupid snakes!" Cacus shook the cell phone violently.

Eek! Martha said.

Help—me! George's voice quivered. *Must—obey—red—bathrobe!*

The phone grew back into a staff.

"Now, behave!" Cacus warned the snakes. "Or I'll turn you two into a fake Gucci handbag!"

Annabeth ran to my side. Together we backed up until we were next to the ladder.

"Our tag game strategy isn't working so well," she noticed. She was breathing heavily. The left sleeve of her T-shirt was smoldering, but otherwise she looked okay. "Any suggestions?"

My ears were ringing. Her voice still sounded like she was underwater.

Wait . . . *under water*.

I looked up the tunnel—all those broken pipes embedded in the rock: waterlines, sewer ducts. Being the son of the sea god, I could sometimes control water. I wondered . . .

"I don't like you!" Cacus yelled. He stalked toward us, smoke pouring from his nostrils. "It's time to end this."

"Hold on," I told Annabeth. I wrapped my free hand around her waist.

I concentrated on finding water above us. It wasn't hard. I felt a dangerous amount of pressure in the city's waterlines, and I summoned it all into the broken pipes.

Cacus towered over us, his mouth glowing like a furnace. "Any last words, demigod?"

"Look up," I told him.

He did.

Note to self: When causing the sewer system of Manhattan to explode, do *not* stand underneath it.

The whole cavern rumbled as a thousand water pipes burst overhead. A not-so-clean waterfall slammed Cacus in the face. I yanked Annabeth out the way, then leaped back into the edge of the torrent, carrying Annabeth with me.

"What are you—?" She made a strangling sound. "Ahhh!"

I'd never attempted this before, but I willed myself to travel upstream like a salmon, jumping from current to current as the water gushed into the cavern. If you've ever tried running up a wet slide, it was kind of like that, except at a ninety-degree angle and with no slide—just water.

Far below I heard Cacus bellowing as millions, maybe even thousands of filthy gallons of water slammed into him. Meanwhile Annabeth alternately shouted, gagged, hit me, called me endearing pet names like, "Idiot! Stupid—dirty—moron—" and topped it all off with, "Kill you!"

Finally we shot out of the ground atop a disgusting geyser and landed safely on the pavement.

Pedestrians and cops backed away, yelling in alarm at our sewage version of Old Faithful. Brakes screeched and cars rear-ended each other as drivers stopped to watch the chaos.

I willed myself dry—a handy trick—but I still smelled pretty bad. Annabeth had old cotton balls stuck in her hair and a wet candy wrapper plastered to her face.

"That," she said, "was horrible!"

bright side," I said, "we're alive."

the caduceus!"

I grimaced. Yeah . . . minor detail. Maybe the giant would drown. Then he'd dissolve and return to Tartarus the way most defeated monsters do, and we could go collect the caduceus.

That sounded reasonable enough.

The geyser receded, followed by the horrendous sound of water draining down the tunnel, like somebody up on Olympus had flushed the godly toilet.

Then a distant snaky voice spoke in my mind. *Gag me*, said George. *Even for me that was disgusting, and I eat rats.*

Incoming! Martha warned. *Oh, no! I think the giant has figured out—*

An explosion shook the street. A beam of blue light shot out of the tunnel, carving a trench up the side of a glass office building, melting windows and vaporizing concrete. The giant climbed from the pit, his velour housecoat steaming, and his face spattered with slime.

He did not look happy. In his hands, the caduceus now resembled a bazooka with snakes wrapped around the barrel and a glowing blue muzzle.

"Okay," Annabeth said faintly. "Um, what is that?"

"That," I guessed, "would be laser mode."

To all of you who live in the Meatpacking District, I apologize. Because of the smoke, debris, and chaos, you probably just call it the Packing District now, since so many of you had to move out.

Still, the real surprise is that we didn't do *more* damage.

Annabeth and I fled as another laser bolt gouged a ditch through the street to our left. Chunks of asphalt rained down like confetti.

Behind us, Cacus yelled, "You ruined my fake Rolexes! They aren't waterproof, you know! For that, you die!"

We kept running. My hope was to get this monster away from innocent mortals, but that's kind of hard to do in the middle of New York. Traffic clogged the streets. Pedestrians screamed and ran in every direction. The two police officers I'd seen earlier were nowhere in sight, maybe swept away by the mob.

"The park!" Annabeth pointed to the elevated tracks of the High Line. "If we can get him off street level—"

BOOM! The laser cut through a nearby food truck. The vendor dove out his service window with a fistful of shish kebabs.

Annabeth and I sprinted for the park stairs. Sirens screamed in the distance, but I didn't want more police involved. Mortal law enforcement would only make things more complicated, and through the Mist, the police might even think Annabeth and I were the problem. You just never knew.

We climbed up to the park. I tried to get my bearings. Under different circumstances, I would've enjoyed the view of the glittering Hudson River and the rooftops of the surrounding neighborhood. The weather was nice. The park's flower beds were bursting with color.

The High Line was empty, though—maybe because it was a workday, or maybe because the visitors were smart and ran when they heard the explosions.

Somewhere below us, Cacus was roaring, cursing, and offering panicked mortals deep discounts on slightly damp Rolexes. I figured we only had a few seconds before he found us.

I scanned the park, hoping for something that would help. All I saw were benches, walkways, and lots of plants. I wished we had a child of Demeter with us. Maybe they could entangle the giant in vines, or turn flowers into ninja throwing stars. I'd never actually seen a child of Demeter do that, but it would be cool.

I looked at Annabeth. "Your turn for a brilliant idea."

"I'm working on it." She was beautiful in combat. I know that's a crazy thing to say, especially after we'd just climbed a sewage waterfall, but her gray eyes sparkled when she was fighting for her life. Her face shone like a goddess's, and believe me, I've seen goddesses. The way her Camp Half-Blood beads rested against her throat— Okay, sorry. Got a little distracted.

She pointed. "There!"

A hundred feet away, the old railroad tracks split and the

elevated platform formed a Y. The shorter piece of the Y was a dead end—part of the park that was still under construction. Stacks of potting soil bags and plant flats sat on the gravel. Jutting over the edge of the railing was the arm of a crane that must've been sitting down at ground level. Far above us, a big metal claw hung from the crane's arm—probably what they'd been using to hoist garden supplies.

Suddenly I understood what Annabeth was planning, and I felt like I was trying to swallow a quarter. "No," I said. "Too dangerous."

Annabeth raised her eyebrow. "Percy, you *know* I rock at grabber-arm games."

That was true. I'd taken her to the arcade at Coney Island, and we'd come back with a sackful of stuffed animals. But this crane was *massive*.

"Don't worry," she promised. "I've supervised bigger equipment on Mount Olympus."

My girlfriend: sophomore honors student, demigod, and—oh, yeah—head architect for redesigning the palace of the gods on Mount Olympus in her spare time.

"But can you operate it?" I asked.

"Cakewalk. Just lure him over there. Keep him occupied while I grab him."

"And then what?"

She smiled in a way that made me glad I wasn't the giant.

"You'll see. If you can snag the caduceus while he's distracted, that would be great."

"Anything else?" I asked. "Would you like fries and a drink, maybe?"

"Shut up, Percy."

"DEATH!" Cacus stormed up the steps and onto the High Line. He spotted us and lumbered over with slow, grim determination.

Annabeth ran. She reached the crane and leaped over the side of the railing, shinnying down the metal arm like it was a tree branch. She disappeared from view.

I raised my sword and faced the giant. His red velour robe was in tatters. He'd lost his slippers. His ginger hair was plastered to his head like a greasy shower cap. He aimed his glowing bazooka.

"George, Martha," I called, hoping they could hear me. "Please change out of laser mode."

We're trying, dear! Martha said.

My stomach hurts, George said. *I think he bruised my tummy.*

I backed up slowly down the dead end tracks, edging toward the crane. Cacus followed. Now that he had me trapped, he seemed in no hurry to kill me. He stopped twenty feet away, just beyond the shadow of the crane's hook. I tried to look cornered and panicked. It wasn't hard.

"So," Cacus growled. "Any last words?"

"Help," I said. *"Yikes. Ouch.* How are those? Oh, and Hermes is a *way* better salesman than you."

"Gah!" Cacus lowered the caduceus laser.

The crane didn't move. Even if Annabeth could get it started, I wondered how she could see her target from down below. I probably should've thought of that sooner.

Cacus pulled the trigger, and suddenly the caduceus changed form. The giant tried to zap me with a credit card–swiping machine, but the only thing that came out was a paper receipt.

Oh, yeah! George yelled in my mind. *One for the snakes!*

"Stupid staff!" Cacus threw down the caduceus in disgust, which was the chance I'd been waiting for. I launched myself forward, snatched the staff, and rolled under the giant's legs.

When I got to my feet, we'd changed positions. Cacus had his back to the crane. Its arm was right behind him, the claw perfectly positioned above his head.

Unfortunately, the crane still wasn't moving. And Cacus still wanted to kill me.

"You put out my fire with that cursed sewage," he growled. "Now you steal my staff."

"Which *you* wrongfully stole," I said.

"It doesn't matter." Cacus cracked his knuckles. "You can't use the staff either. I'll simply kill you with my bare hands."

The crane shifted, slowly and almost silently. I realized there were mirrors fixed along the side of the arm—like rearview mirrors to guide the operator. And reflected in one of those mirrors were Annabeth's gray eyes.

The claw opened and began to drop.

I smiled at the giant. "Actually, Cacus, I have another secret weapon."

The giant's eyes lit up with greed. "Another weapon? I will steal it! I will copy it and sell the knockoffs for a profit! What is this secret weapon?"

"Her name is Annabeth," I said. "And she's one of a kind."

The claw dropped, smacking Cacus on the head and knocking him to the ground. While the giant was dazed, the claw closed around his chest and lifted him into the air.

"Wh—what is this?" The giant came to his senses twenty feet up. "Put me down!"

He squirmed uselessly and tried to blow fire, but only managed to cough up some mud.

Annabeth swung the crane arm back and forth, building momentum as the giant cursed and struggled. I was afraid the whole crane would tip over, but Annabeth's control was perfect. She swung the arm one last time and opened the claw when the giant was at the top of his arc.

"Aahhhhhhhhh!" The giant sailed over the rooftops, straight over Chelsea Piers, and began falling toward the Hudson River.

"George, Martha," I said. "Do you think you could manage laser mode just once more for me?"

With pleasure, George said.

The caduceus turned into a wicked high-tech bazooka.

I took aim at the falling giant and yelled, "Pull!"

The caduceus blasted its beam of blue light, and the giant disintegrated into a beautiful starburst.

That, George said, *was excellent. May I have a rat now?*

I have to agree with George, Martha said. *A rat would be lovely.*

"You've earned it," I said. "But first we'd better check on Annabeth."

She met me at the steps of the park, grinning like crazy.

"Was that amazing?" she demanded.

"That was amazing," I agreed. It's hard to pull off a romantic kiss when you're both drenched in muck, but we gave it our best shot.

When I finally came up for air, I said, "Rats."

"Rats?" she asked.

"For the snakes," I said. "And then—"

"Oh, gods." She pulled out her phone and checked the time. "It's almost five. We have to get the caduceus back to Hermes!"

———

The surface streets were clogged with emergency vehicles and minor accidents, so we took the subway back. Besides, the subway had rats. Without going into gruesome details, I can tell you that George and Martha helped out with the vermin problem.

As we traveled north, they curled around the caduceus and dozed contentedly with bulging bellies.

We met Hermes by the Atlas statue at Rockefeller Center. (The statue, by the way, looks nothing like the real Atlas, but that's another story.)

"Thank the Fates!" Hermes cried. "I'd just about given up hope!"

He took the caduceus and patted the heads of his sleepy snakes. "There, there, my friends. You're home now."

Zzzzz, said Martha.

Yummy, George murmured in his sleep.

Hermes sighed with relief. "Thank you, Percy."

Annabeth cleared her throat.

"Oh, yes," the god added, "and you, too, girl. I just have time to finish my deliveries! But what happened with Cacus?"

We told him the story. When I related what Cacus had said about someone else giving him the idea to steal the caduceus, and about the gods having other enemies, Hermes's face darkened.

"Cacus wanted to cut the gods' communication lines, did he?" Hermes mused. "That's ironic, considering Zeus has been threatening . . ."

His voice trailed off.

"What?" Annabeth asked. "Zeus has been threatening what?"

"Nothing," Hermes said.

It was obviously a lie, but I'd learned that it's best not to confront gods when they lie to your face. They tend to turn you into small fuzzy mammals or potted plants.

"Okay . . ." I said. "Any idea what Cacus meant about other enemies, or who would want him to steal your caduceus?"

Hermes fidgeted. "Oh, could be any number of enemies. We gods *do* have many."

"Hard to believe," Annabeth said.

Hermes nodded. Apparently he didn't catch the sarcasm, or he had other things on his mind. I got the feeling the giant's warnings would come back to haunt us sooner or later, but Hermes obviously wasn't going to enlighten us now.

The god managed a smile. "At any rate, well done, both of you! Now I must be going. So many stops—"

"There's the small matter of my reward," I reminded him.

Annabeth frowned. "What reward?"

"It's our one-month anniversary," I said. "Surely you didn't forget."

She opened her mouth and closed it again. I don't leave her speechless very often. I have to enjoy those rare moments.

"Ah, yes, your reward." Hermes looked us up and down. "I think we'll have to start with new clothes. Manhattan sewage is not a look you can pull off. Then the rest should be easy. God of travel, at your service."

"What is he talking about?" Annabeth asked.

"A special surprise for dinner," I said. "I *did* promise."

Hermes rubbed his hands. "Say good-bye, George and Martha."

Good-bye, George and Martha, said George sleepily.

Zzz, said Martha.

"I may not see you for a while, Percy," Hermes warned. "But . . . well, enjoy tonight."

He made that sound so ominous, I wondered again what he wasn't telling me. Then he snapped his fingers, and the world dissolved around us.

———

Our table was ready. The maître d' seated us on a rooftop terrace with a view of the lights of Paris and the boats on the River Seine. The Eiffel Tower glowed in the distance.

I was wearing a suit. I hope someone got a picture, because I don't *wear* suits. Thankfully, Hermes had magically arranged this. Otherwise I couldn't have tied the tie. Hopefully I looked okay, because Annabeth looked stunning. She wore a dark green sleeveless dress that showed off her long blond hair and her slim athletic figure. Her camp necklace had been replaced by a string of gray pearls that matched her eyes.

The waiter brought fresh-baked bread and cheese, a bottle of sparkling water for Annabeth, and a Coke with ice for me (because I'm a barbarian). We dined on a bunch of stuff I couldn't even pronounce—but all of it was great. It was almost half an hour before Annabeth got over her shock and spoke.

"This is . . . incredible."

"Only the best for you," I said. "And you thought I forgot."

"You *did* forget, Seaweed Brain." But her smile told me she wasn't really mad. "Nice save, though. I'm impressed."

"I have my moments."

"You certainly do." She reached across the table and took my hand. Her expression turned serious. "Any idea why Hermes acted so nervous? I got the feeling something bad was happening on Olympus."

I shook my head. *I may not see you for a while*, the god had said, almost like he was warning me about something to come.

"Let's just enjoy tonight," I said. "Hermes will be teleporting us back at midnight."

"Time for a walk along the river," Annabeth suggested. "And Percy . . . feel free to start planning our two-month anniversary."

"Oh, gods." I felt panicky at the thought, but also really good. I'd survived a month as Annabeth's boyfriend, so I guess I hadn't screwed things up too badly. In fact, I'd never been happier. If she saw a future for us—if she was still planning to be with me next month, then that was good enough for me.

"How about we go for that walk?" I pulled out the credit card Hermes had tucked in my pocket—a black metal Olympus Express—and set it on the table. "I want to explore Paris with a beautiful girl."

INTERVIEW WITH GEORGE AND MARTHA, HERMES'S SNAKES

It's such an honor to speak with you. You're quite famous, you know.

GEORGE: *That's right, buddy. We are VISs—very important snakes. Without us, Hermes's staff would be nothing but a boring old branch.*

MARTHA: *Shhhh . . . he might hear you. Hermes, if you're listening, we think you're wonderful.*

GEORGE: *Yes, we're very glad you caught us, Hermes. Please don't stop feeding us.*

What's it like to work for Hermes?

MARTHA: *We work* with *Hermes, dear. Not* for.

GEORGE: *Yeah, just because he caught us and made us part of his caduceus doesn't mean he owns us. We're his constant companions and he'd be bored without us. And he'd look quite silly without his caduceus, now, wouldn't he?*

What's the best part of your job?

MARTHA: *I like talking with the young demigods. So sweet, those children. It's sad to see when they turn bad, though. . . .*

GEORGE: *That Kronos business was a mess, but let's not talk about the sad stuff. Let's talk about the fun stuff, like lasers and traveling the world with Hermes.*

Yes, what do you do while Hermes is off delivering packages, acting as a patron to travelers and thieves, and being a messenger of the gods?

GEORGE: *Well, it's not like we're useless, you know. What, you think we just hang around and sunbathe on the caduceus all day?*

MARTHA: *George, hush, you're being rude.*

GEORGE: *But he should know that we're quite indispensible.*

MARTHA: *What George means is that we do a lot for Hermes. First of all, we provide moral support to Hermes, and I'd like to think that our soothing presence helps young demigods when Hermes is delivering so-so news.*

GEORGE: *We do cooler stuff than that. Hermes can use the caduceus as a cattle prod, a laser, even a cell phone, and when he does, yours truly is the antennae.*

MARTHA: *And when he delivers packages and customers need to sign their receipts, I—*

GEORGE: *She's the pen, I'm the notepad.*

MARTHA: *George, don't interrupt.*

GEORGE: *All I'm saying is that Hermes couldn't do his job without us!*

Phone, notepad, pen—it sounds like you guys wear a lot of hats.

GEORGE: *Did you say* rats?

MARTHA: *No, no, he said* hats. *Because we do a lot of different things, we wear a lot of different* hats.

GEORGE: *Rats are delicious.*

MARTHA: *Not rats with an R, HATS with an—*

GEORGE: *All this talk about rats is making me hungry. Let's go get lunch.*

UNDERGROUND CAVERN ESCAPE

THALIA

HAL

LUKE

CAMP HALF~BLOOD

ANNABETH

PERCY

PIPER

LEO

JASON

LEO VALDEZ
AND THE
QUEST
FOR
BUFORD

LEO BLAMED THE WINDEX. He should've known better. Now his entire project—two months of work—might literally blow up in his face.

He stormed around Bunker 9, cursing himself for being so stupid, while his friends tried to calm him down.

"It's okay," Jason said. "We're here to help."

"Just tell us what happened," Piper urged.

Thank goodness they'd answered his distress call so quickly. Leo couldn't turn to anyone else. Having his best friends at his side made him feel better, though he wasn't sure they could stop the disaster.

Jason looked cool and confident as usual—all surfer-dude handsome with his blond hair and sky-blue eyes. The scar on his mouth and the sword at his side gave him a rugged appearance, like he could handle anything.

Piper stood next to him in her jeans and orange camp T-shirt.

Her long brown hair was braided on one side. Her dagger Katoptris gleamed at her belt. Despite the situation, her multicolored eyes sparkled like she was trying to suppress a smile. Now that Jason and she were officially together, Piper looked like that a lot.

Leo took a deep breath. "Okay, guys. This is *serious*. Buford's gone. If we don't get him back, this whole place is going to explode."

Piper's eyes lost some of that smiley sparkle. "Explode? Um . . . okay. Just calm down and tell us who Buford is."

She probably didn't do it on purpose, but Piper had this child-of-Aphrodite power called *charmspeak* that made her voice hard to ignore. Leo felt his muscles relaxing. His mind cleared a little.

"Fine," he said. "Come here."

He led them across the hangar floor, carefully skirting some of his more dangerous projects. In his two months at Camp Half-Blood, Leo had spent most of his time at Bunker 9. After all, he'd rediscovered the secret workshop. Now it was like a second home to him. But he knew his friends still felt uncomfortable here.

He couldn't blame them. Built into the side of a limestone cliff deep in the woods, the bunker was part weapons depot, part machine shop, and part underground safe house, with a little bit of Area 51–style craziness thrown in for good measure. Rows of workbenches stretched into the darkness. Tool cabinets, storage closets, cages full of welding equipment, and stacks of construction material made a labyrinth of aisles so vast, Leo figured he'd only explored about ten percent of it so far. Overhead ran a series of catwalks and pneumatic tubes for delivering supplies, plus a high-tech lighting and sound system that Leo was just starting to figure out.

A large magical banner hung over the center of the production floor. Leo had recently discovered how to change the display, like the Times Square JumboTron, so now the banner read: *Merry Christmas! All your presents belong to Leo!*

He ushered his friends to the central staging area. Decades ago, Leo's metallic friend Festus the bronze dragon had been created here. Now, Leo was slowly assembling his pride and joy—the *Argo II*.

At the moment, it didn't look like much. The keel was laid—a length of Celestial bronze curved like an archer's bow, two hundred feet from bow to stern. The lowest hull planks had been set in place, forming a shallow bowl held together by scaffolding. Masts lay to one side, ready for positioning. The bronze dragon figurehead—formerly the head of Festus—sat nearby, carefully wrapped in velvet, waiting to be installed in its place of honor.

Most of Leo's time had been spent in the middle of the ship, at the base of the hull, where he was building the engine that would run the warship.

He climbed the scaffolding and jumped into the hull. Jason and Piper followed.

"See?" Leo said.

Fixed to the keel, the engine apparatus looked like a high-tech jungle gym made from pipes, pistons, bronze gears, magical disks, steam vents, electric wires, and a million other magical and mechanical pieces. Leo slid inside and pointed out the combustion chamber.

It was a thing of beauty, a bronze sphere the size of a basketball, its surface bristling with glass cylinders so it looked like a mechanical starburst. Gold wires ran from the ends of the cylinders, connecting to various parts of the engine. Each cylinder was filled with a different magical and highly dangerous substance. The central sphere had a digital clock display that read *66:21*. The maintenance panel was open. Inside, the core was empty.

"There's your problem," Leo announced.

Jason scratched his head. "Uh . . . what are we looking at?"

Leo thought it was pretty obvious, but Piper looked confused too.

"Okay," Leo sighed, "you want the full explanation or the short explanation?"

"Short," Piper and Jason said in unison.

Leo gestured to the empty core. "The syncopator goes here. It's a multi-access gyro-valve to regulate flow. The dozen glass tubes on the outside? Those are filled with powerful, dangerous stuff. That glowing red one is Lemnos fire from my dad's forges. This murky stuff here? That's water from the River Styx. The stuff in the tubes is going to power the ship, right? Like radioactive rods in a nuclear reactor. But the mix ratio has to be controlled, and the timer is already operational."

Leo tapped the digital clock, which now read *65:15*. "That means without the syncopator, this stuff is all going to vent into the chamber at the same time, in sixty-five minutes. At that point, we'll get a very nasty reaction."

Jason and Piper stared at him. Leo wondered if he'd been speaking English. Sometimes when he was agitated he slipped into Spanish, like his mom used to do in her workshop. But he was pretty sure he'd used English.

"Um . . ." Piper cleared her throat. "Could you make the short explanation shorter?"

Leo palm-smacked his forehead. "Fine. One hour. Fluids mix. Bunker goes ka-boom. One square mile of forest turns into a smoking crater."

"Oh," Piper said in a small voice. "Can't you just . . . turn it off?"

"Gee, I didn't think of that!" Leo said. "Let me just hit this switch and— *No*, Piper. I can't turn it off. This is a tricky piece of machinery. Everything has to be assembled in a certain order in a certain amount of time. Once the combustion chamber is rigged, like this, you can't just leave all those tubes sitting there.

The engine has to be put into motion. The countdown clock started automatically, and I've got to install the syncopator before the fuel goes critical. Which would be fine except . . . well, I lost the syncopator."

Jason folded his arms. "You *lost* it. Don't you have an extra? Can't you pull one out of your tool belt?"

Leo shook his head. His magic tool belt could produce a lot of great stuff. Any kind of common tool—hammers, screwdrivers, bolt cutters, whatever—Leo could pull out of the pockets just by thinking about it. But the belt couldn't fabricate complicated devices or magic items.

"The syncopator took me a week to make," he said. "And yes, I made a spare. I always do. But that's lost too. They were both in Buford's drawers."

"Who is Buford?" Piper asked. "And why are you storing syncopators in his drawers?"

Leo rolled his eyes. "Buford is a table."

"A table," Jason repeated. "Named Buford."

"Yes, a table." Leo wondered if his friends were losing their hearing. "A magic walking table. About three feet high, mahogany top, bronze base, three movable legs. I saved him from one of the supply closets and got him in working order. He's just like the tables my dad has in his workshop. Awesome helper; carries all my important machine parts."

"So what happened to him?" Piper asked.

Leo felt a lump rising in his throat. The guilt was almost too much. "I—I got careless. I polished him with Windex, and . . . he ran away."

Jason looked like he was trying to figure out an equation. "Let me get this straight. Your table ran away . . . because you polished him with Windex."

"I know, I'm an idiot!" Leo moaned. "A brilliant idiot, but still an idiot. Buford *hates* being polished with Windex. It has to be Lemon Pledge with extra-moisturizing formula. I was distracted. I thought maybe just once he wouldn't notice. Then I turned around for a while to install the combustion tubes, and when I looked for Buford . . ."

Leo pointed to the giant open doors of the bunker. "He was gone. Little trail of oil and bolts leading outside. He could be anywhere by now, and he's got both syncopators!"

Piper glanced at the digital clock. "So . . . we have exactly one hour to find your runaway table, get back your synco-whatsit, and install it in this engine, or the *Argo II* explodes, destroying Bunker Nine and most of the woods."

"Basically," Leo said.

Jason frowned. "We should alert the other campers. We might have to evacuate them."

"No!" Leo's voice broke. "Look, the explosion won't destroy the whole camp. Just the woods. I'm pretty sure. Like sixty-five percent sure."

"Well, that's a relief," Piper muttered.

"Besides," Leo said, "we don't have time, and I—I *can't* tell the others. If they find out how badly I've messed up . . ."

Jason and Piper looked at each other. The clock display changed to *59:00*.

"Fine," Jason said. "But we'd better hurry."

As they trudged through the woods, the sun started to set. The camp's weather was magically controlled, so it wasn't freezing and snowing like it was in the rest of Long Island, but still Leo could tell it was late December. In the shadows of the huge oak trees, the air was cold and damp. The mossy ground squished under their feet.

Leo was tempted to summon fire in his hand. He'd gotten better at that since coming to camp, but he knew the nature spirits in the woods didn't like fire. He didn't want to be yelled at by any more dryads.

Christmas Eve. Leo couldn't believe it was here already. He'd been working so hard in Bunker 9, he'd hardly noticed the weeks passing. Usually around the holidays he would be goofing around, pranking his friends, dressing up like Taco Claus (his personal invention), and leaving carne asada tacos in people's socks and sleeping bags, or pouring eggnog down his friends' shirts, or making up inappropriate lyrics to Christmas carols. This year, he was all serious and hardworking. Any teacher he'd ever had would laugh if Leo described himself that way.

Thing was, Leo had never cared so much about a project before. The *Argo II* had to be ready by June if they were going to start their big quest on time. And while June seemed a long way away, Leo knew he'd barely have time to make the deadline. Even with the entire Hephaestus cabin helping him, constructing a magic flying warship was a huge task. It made launching a NASA spaceship look easy. They'd had so many setbacks, but all Leo could think about was getting the ship finished. It would be his masterpiece.

Also, he wanted to get the dragon figurehead installed. He missed his old friend Festus, who'd literally crashed and burned on their last quest. Even if Festus would never be the same again, Leo hoped he could reactivate his brain by using the ship's engines. If Leo could give Festus a second life, he wouldn't feel so bad.

But none of that would happen if the combustion chamber exploded. It would be game over. No ship. No Festus. No quest. Leo would have no one to blame but himself. He really hated Windex.

Jason knelt at the banks of a stream. He pointed to some marks in the mud. "Do those look like table tracks?"

"Or a raccoon," Leo suggested.

Jason frowned. "With no toes?"

"Piper?" Leo asked. "What do you think?"

She sighed. "Just because I'm Native American doesn't mean I can track furniture through the wilderness." She deepened her voice: "'Yes, *kemosabe*. A three-legged table passed this way an hour ago.' Heck, I don't know."

"Okay, jeez," Leo said.

Piper was half Cherokee, half Greek goddess. Some days it was hard to tell which side of her family she was more sensitive about.

"It's probably a table," Jason decided. "Which means Buford went across this stream."

Suddenly the water gurgled. A girl in a shimmering blue dress rose to the surface. She had stringy green hair, blue lips, and pale skin, so she looked like a drowning victim. Her eyes were wide with alarm.

"Could you be any louder?" she hissed. "They'll hear you!"

Leo blinked. He never got used to this—nature spirits just popping up out of trees and streams and whatnot.

"Are you a naiad?" he asked.

"Shh! They'll kill us all! They're right over *there*!" She pointed behind her, into the trees on the other side of the stream. Unfortunately, that was the direction Buford seemed to have walked.

"Okay," Piper said gently, kneeling next to the water. "We

appreciate the warning. What's your name?"

The naiad looked like she wanted to bolt, but Piper's voice was hard to resist.

"Brooke," the blue girl said reluctantly.

"Brooke the brook?" Jason asked.

Piper swatted his leg. "Okay, Brooke. I'm Piper. We won't let anyone harm you. Just tell us who you're afraid of."

The naiad's face became more agitated. The water boiled around her. "My crazy cousins. You can't stop them. They'll tear you apart. None of us is safe! Now go away. I have to hide!"

Brooke melted into water.

Piper stood. "Crazy cousins?" She frowned at Jason. "Any idea what she was talking about?"

Jason shook his head. "Maybe we should keep our voices down."

Leo stared at the stream. He was trying to figure what was so horrible that it could tear apart a river spirit. How do you tear up water? Whatever it was, he didn't want to meet it.

Yet he could see Buford's tracks on the opposite bank—little square prints in the mud, leading in the direction the naiad had warned them about.

"We have to follow the trail, right?" he said, mostly to convince himself. "I mean . . . we're heroes and stuff. We can handle whatever it is. Right?"

Jason drew his sword—a wicked Roman-style gladius with an Imperial gold blade. "Right. Of course."

Piper unsheathed her dagger. She stared into the blade as if hoping Katoptris would show her a helpful vision. Sometimes the dagger did that. But if she saw anything important, she didn't say.

"Crazy cousins," she muttered. "Here we come."

———

There was no more talking as they followed the table tracks deeper into the woods. The birds were silent. No monsters growled. It was as if all the other living creatures in the woods had been smart enough to leave.

Finally they came to a clearing the size of a mall parking lot. The sky overhead was heavy and gray. The grass was dry yellow, and the ground was scarred with pits and trenches as if someone had done some crazy driving with construction equipment. In the center of the clearing stood a pile of boulders about thirty feet tall.

"Oh," Piper said. "This isn't good."

"Why?" Leo asked.

"It's bad luck to be here," Jason said. "This is the battle site."

Leo scowled. "What battle?"

Piper raised her eyebrows. "How can you not know about it? The other campers talk about this place all the time."

"Been a little busy," Leo said.

He tried not to feel bitter about it, but he'd missed out on a lot of regular camp stuff—the trireme fights, the chariot races, flirting with the girls. That was the worst part. Leo finally had an "in" with the hottest girls at camp, since Piper was the senior counselor for Aphrodite cabin, and he was too busy for her to fix him up. Sad.

"The Battle of the Labyrinth." Piper kept her voice down, but she explained to Leo how the pile of rocks used to be called Zeus's Fist, back when it looked like something, not just a pile of rocks. There'd been an entrance to a magical labyrinth here, and a big army of monsters had come through it to invade camp. The campers won—obviously, since camp was still here—but it had been a hard battle. Several demigods had died. The clearing was still considered cursed.

"Great," Leo grumbled. "Buford has to run to the most dangerous part of the woods. He couldn't just, like, run to the beach or a burger shop."

"Speaking of which . . ." Jason studied the ground. "How are we going to track him? There's no trail here."

Though Leo would've preferred to stay in the cover of the trees, he followed his friends into the clearing. They searched for table tracks, but as they made their way to the pile of boulders they found nothing. Leo pulled a watch from his tool belt and strapped it to his wrist. Roughly forty minutes until the big *ka-boom*.

"If I had more time," he said, "I could make a tracking device, but—"

"Does Buford have a round tabletop?" Piper interrupted. "With little steam vents sticking up on one side?"

Leo stared at her. "How did you know?"

"Because he's right over there." She pointed.

Sure enough, Buford was waddling toward the far end of the clearing, steam puffing from his vents. As they watched, he disappeared into the trees.

"That was easy." Jason started to follow, but Leo held him back.

The hairs on the back of Leo's neck stood up. He wasn't sure why. Then he realized he could hear voices from the woods on their left. "Someone's coming!"

He pulled his friends behind the boulders.

Jason whispered, "Leo—"

"Shh!"

A dozen barefoot girls skipped into the clearing. They were teenagers with tunic-style dresses of loose purple and red silk. Their hair was tangled with leaves, and most wore laurel wreaths. Some carried strange staffs that looked like torches. The girls laughed and swung each other around, tumbling in the grass and spinning like they were dizzy. They were all really gorgeous, but Leo wasn't tempted to flirt.

Piper sighed. "They're just nymphs, Leo."

Leo gestured frantically at her to stay down. He whispered, "Crazy cousins!"

Piper's eyes widened.

As the nymphs got closer, Leo started to notice odd details about them. Their staffs weren't torches. They were twisted wooden branches, each topped with a giant pinecone, and some were wrapped with living snakes. The girls' laurel wreaths weren't wreaths, either. Their hair was braided with tiny vipers. The girls smiled and laughed and sang in Ancient Greek as they stumbled around the glade. They appeared to be having a great time, but their voices were tinged with a sort of wild ferocity. If leopards could sing, Leo thought they would sound like this.

"Are they drunk?" Jason whispered.

Leo frowned. The girls *did* act like that, but he thought there was something else going on. He was glad the nymphs hadn't seen them yet.

Then things got complicated. In the woods to their right, something roared. The trees rustled, and a drakon burst into the clearing, looking sleepy and irritated, as if the nymphs' singing had woken it up.

Leo had seen plenty of monsters in the woods. The camp intentionally stocked them as a challenge to campers. But this was bigger and scarier than most.

The drakon was about the size of a subway car. It had no

wings, but its mouth bristled with daggerlike teeth. Flames curled from its nostrils. Silvery scales covered its body like polished chain mail. When the drakon saw the nymphs, it roared again and shot flames into the sky.

The girls didn't seem to notice. They kept doing cartwheels and laughing and playfully pushing each other around.

"We've got to help them," Piper whispered. "They'll be killed!"

"Hold on," Leo said.

"Leo," Jason chided. "We're heroes. We can't let innocent girls—"

"Just chill!" Leo insisted. Something bothered him about these girls—a story he only half remembered. As counselor for Hephaestus cabin, Leo made it his business to read up on magic items, just in case he needed to build them someday. He was sure he'd read something about pinecone staffs wrapped with snakes. "Watch."

Finally one of the girls noticed the drakon. She squealed in delight, as if she'd spotted a cute puppy. She skipped toward the monster and the other girls followed, singing and laughing, which seemed to confuse the drakon. It probably wasn't used to its prey being so cheerful.

A nymph in a blood-red dress did a cartwheel and landed in front of the drakon. "Are you Dionysus?" she asked hopefully.

It seemed like a stupid question. True, Leo had never met

Dionysus, but he was pretty sure the god of wine wasn't a fire-breathing drakon.

The monster blasted fire at the girl's feet. She simply danced out of the kill zone. The drakon lunged and caught her arm in its jaws. Leo winced, sure the nymph's limb would be amputated right before his eyes, but she yanked it free, along with several broken drakon teeth. Her arm was perfectly fine. The drakon made a sound somewhere between a growl and a whimper.

"Naughty!" the girl scolded. She turned to her cheerful friends. "Not Dionysus! He must join our party!"

A dozen nymphs squealed in delight and surrounded the monster.

Piper caught her breath. "What are they—oh, gods. No!"

Leo didn't usually feel sorry for monsters, but what happened next was truly horrifying. The girls threw themselves at the drakon. Their cheerful laughter turned into vicious snarling. They attacked with their pinecone staffs, with fingernails that turned into long white talons, with teeth that elongated into wolfish fangs.

The monster blew fire and stumbled, trying to get away, but the teenage girls were too much for him. The nymphs ripped and tore until the drakon slowly crumbled into powder, its spirit returning to Tartarus.

Jason made a gulping sound. Leo had seen his friend in all sorts of dangerous situations, but he'd never seen Jason look quite so pale.

Piper was shielding her eyes, muttering, "Oh, gods. Oh, gods."

Leo tried to keep his own voice from trembling. "I read about these nymphs. They're followers of Dionysus. I forget what they're called—"

"Maenads." Piper shivered. "I've heard of them. I thought they only existed in ancient times. They attended Dionysus's parties. When they got too excited . . ."

She pointed toward the clearing. She didn't need to say more. Brooke the naiad had warned them. Her crazy cousins ripped their victims to pieces.

"We have to get out of here," Jason said.

"But they're between us and Buford!" Leo whispered. "And we've only got—" He checked his watch. "Thirty minutes to get the syncopator installed!"

"Maybe I can fly us over to Buford." Jason shut his eyes tight.

Leo knew Jason had controlled the wind before—just one of the advantages of being the über-cool son of Zeus—but this time, nothing happened.

Jason shook his head. "I don't know . . . the air feels agitated. Maybe those nymphs are messing things up. Even the wind spirits are too nervous to get close."

Leo glanced back the way they'd come. "We'll have to retreat to the woods. If we can skirt around the Maenads—"

"Guys," Piper squeaked in alarm.

Leo looked up. He hadn't noticed the Maenads approaching, climbing the rocks with absolute silence even creepier than their laughter. They peered down from the tops of the boulders, smiling prettily, their fingernails and teeth back to normal. Vipers coiled through their hair.

"Hello!" The girl in the blood-red dress beamed at Leo. "Are you Dionysus?"

———

There was only one answer to that.

"Yes!" Leo yelped. "Absolutely. I am Dionysus."

He got to his feet and tried to match the girl's smile.

The nymph clapped her hands in delight. "Wonderful! My lord Dionysus? Really?"

Jason and Piper rose, weapons ready, but Leo hoped it didn't come to a fight. He'd seen how fast these nymphs could move. If they decided to go into food-processor mode, Leo doubted he and his friends would stand a chance.

The Maenads giggled and danced and pushed each other around. Several fell off the rocks and landed hard on the ground. That didn't seem to bother them. They just got up and kept frolicking.

Piper nudged Leo in the ribs. "Um, Lord Dionysus, what are you doing?"

"Everything's cool." Leo looked at his friends like, *Everything's really, really not cool.* "The Maenads are my attendants. I love these guys."

The Maenads cheered and twirled around him. Several produced goblets from thin air and began to chug . . . whatever was inside.

The girl in red looked uncertainly at Piper and Jason. "Lord Dionysus, are these two sacrifices for the party? Should we rip them to pieces?"

"No, no!" Leo said. "Great offer, but, um, you know, maybe we should start small. With, like, introductions."

The girl narrowed her eyes. "Surely you remember me, my lord. I am Babette."

"Um, right!" Leo said. "Babette! Of course."

"And these are Buffy, Muffy, Bambi, Candy—" Babette rattled off a bunch more names that all kind of blended together. Leo glanced at Piper, wondering if this was some sort of Aphrodite joke. These nymphs could've totally fit in with Piper's cabin. But Piper looked like she was trying not to scream. That might've been because two of the Maenads were running their hands over Jason's shoulders and giggling.

Babette stepped closer to Leo. She smelled like pine needles. Her curly dark hair spilled over her shoulders and freckles splashed across her nose. A wreath of coral snakes writhed across her forehead.

Nature spirits usually had a greenish tinge to their skin from chlorophyll, but these Maenads looked like their blood was cherry Kool-Aid. Their eyes were severely bloodshot. Their lips were redder than normal. Their skin was webbed with bright capillaries.

"An interesting form you've chosen, my lord." Babette inspected Leo's face and hair. "Youthful. Cute, I suppose. Yet . . . somewhat scrawny and short."

"Scrawny and short?" Leo bit back a few choice replies. "Well, you know. I was going for *cute*, mostly."

The other Maenads circled Leo, smiling and humming. Under normal circumstances, being surrounded by hot girls would've been *totally* okay with Leo, but not this time. He couldn't forget how the Maenads' teeth and nails had grown just before they tore the drakon to shreds.

"So, my lord." Babette ran her fingers down Leo's arm. "Where have you been? We've searched for so long!"

"Where have I—?" Leo thought furiously. He knew Dionysus used to work as the director of Camp Half-Blood before Leo's time. Then the god had been recalled to Mount Olympus to help deal with the giants. But where did Dionysus hang out these days? Leo had no idea. "Oh, you know. I've been doing, um, wine stuff. Yeah. Red wine. White wine. All those other kinds of wine. Love that wine. I've been so busy working—"

"Work!" Muffy the Maenad shrieked, pressing her hands over her ears.

"Work!" Buffy wiped her tongue as if trying to scrub away the horrible word.

The other Maenads dropped their goblets and ran in circles, yelling "Work! Sacrilege! Kill work!" Some began to grow long claws. Other slammed their heads against the boulders, which seemed to hurt the boulders more than their heads.

"He means partying!" Piper shouted. "Partying! Lord Dionysus has been busy partying all over the world."

Slowly, the Maenads began to calm down.

"Party?" Bambi asked cautiously.

"Party!" Candy sighed with relief.

"Yeah!" Leo wiped the sweat off his hands. He shot Piper a grateful look. "Ha-ha. Partying. Right. I've been *so* busy partying."

Babette kept smiling, but not in such a friendly way. She fixed her gaze on Piper. "Who is this one, my lord? A recruit for the Maenads, perhaps?"

"Oh," Leo said. "She's my, uh, party planner."

"Party!" yelled another Maenad, possibly Trixie.

"What a shame." Babette's fingernails began to grow. "We can't allow mortals to witness our sacred revels."

"But I *could* be a recruit!" Piper said quickly. "Do you guys have a website? Or a list of requirements? Er, do you have to be drunk all the time?"

"Drunk!" Babette said. "Don't be silly. We're underage Maenads. We haven't graduated to wine yet. What would our parents think?"

"You have *parents*?" Jason shrugged the Maenads' hands off his shoulders.

"Not drunk!" Candy yelled. She turned in a dizzy circle and fell down, spilling white frothy liquid from her goblet.

Jason cleared his throat. "So . . . what are you guys drinking if it isn't wine?"

Babette laughed. "The beverage of the season! Behold the power of the thyrsus rod!"

She slammed her pinecone staff against the ground and a white geyser bubbled up. "Eggnog!"

Maenads rushed forward to fill their goblets.

"Merry Christmas!" one yelled.

"Party!" another said.

"Kill everything!" said a third.

Piper took a step back. "You're . . . drunk on eggnog?"

"Whee!" Buffy sloshed her eggnog and gave Leo a frothy grin. "Kill things! With a sprinkle of nutmeg!"

Leo decided never to drink eggnog again.

"But enough talk, my lord," Babette said. "You've been naughty, keeping yourself hidden! You changed your e-mail and phone number. One might think the great Dionysus was trying to avoid his Maenads!"

Jason removed another girl's hands from his shoulders. "Can't imagine why the great Dionysus would do that."

Babette sized up Jason. "This one is a sacrifice, obviously. We should start the festivities by ripping him apart. The party planner girl can prove herself by helping us!"

"Or," Leo said, "we could start with some appetizers. Crispy Cheese 'n' Wieners. Taquitos. Maybe some chips and queso. And . . . wait, I know! We need a table to put them on."

Babette's smile wavered. The snakes hissed around her pine-cone staff. "A table?"

"Cheese 'n' Wieners?" Trixie added hopefully.

"Yeah, a table!" Leo snapped his fingers and pointed toward the end of the clearing. "You know what—I think I saw one walking that way. Why don't you guys wait here, and drink some eggnog or whatever, and my friends and I will go get the table. We'll be right back!"

He started to leave, but two of the Maenads pushed him back. The push didn't seem exactly playful.

Babette's eyes turned an even deeper red. "Why is my lord Dionysus so interested in furniture? Where is your leopard? And your wine cup?"

Leo gulped. "Yeah. Wine cup. Silly me." He reached into his tool bag. He prayed it would produce a wine cup for him, but that wasn't exactly a tool. He grabbed something, pulled it out, and found himself holding a lug wrench.

"Hey, look at that," he said weakly. "There's some godly magic right there, huh? What's a party without . . . a lug wrench?"

The Maenads stared at him. Some frowned. Others were cross-eyed from the eggnog.

Jason stepped to his side. "Hey, um, Dionysus . . . maybe we should talk. Like, in private. You know . . . about party stuff."

"We'll be right back!" Piper announced. "Just wait here, you guys. Okay?"

Her voice was almost electric with charmspeak, but the Maenads didn't appear moved.

"No, you will stay." Babette's eyes bored into Leo's. "You do not act like Dionysus. Those who fail to honor the god, those who *dare* to work instead of partying—they must be ripped apart. And anyone who dares to impersonate the god, he must die even more painfully."

"Wine!" Leo yelped. "Did I mention how much I love wine?"

Babette didn't look convinced. "If you are the god of parties, you will know the order of our revelries. Prove it! Lead us!"

Leo felt trapped. He'd once been stuck in a cave on top of Pikes Peak, surrounded by a pack of werewolves. Another time he'd been stuck in an abandoned factory with a family of evil Cyclopes. But this—standing in an open clearing with a dozen pretty girls—was *much* worse.

"Sure!" His voice squeaked. "Revelries. So we start with the Hokey Pokey—"

Trixie snarled. "No, my lord. The Hokey Pokey is *second*."

"Right," Leo said. "First is the limbo contest, *then* the Hokey Pokey. Then, um, pin the tail on the donkey—"

"Wrong!" Babette's eyes turned completely red. The Kool-Aid darkened in her veins, making a web of red lines like ivy under her skin. "Last chance, and I'll even give you a hint. We begin by singing the Bacchanalian Jingle. You *do* remember it, don't you?"

Leo's tongue felt like sandpaper.

Piper put her hand on his arm. "Of course he remembers it." Her eyes said, *Run.*

Jason's knuckles turned white on the hilt of his sword.

Leo hated singing. He cleared his throat and started warbling the first thing that came into his head—something he'd watched online while he worked on the *Argo II.*

After a few lines, Candy hissed. "That is not the Bacchanalian Jingle! That is the theme song for *Psych!*"

"Kill the unbelievers!" Babette screamed.

———·—·———

Leo knew an exit cue when he heard one.

He pulled a reliable trick. From his tool belt, he grabbed a flask of oil and splashed it in an arc in front of him, dousing the Maenads. He didn't want to hurt anyone, but he reminded himself these girls weren't human. They were nature spirits bent on ripping him apart. He summoned fire into his hands and set the oil ablaze.

A wall of flames engulfed the nymphs. Jason and Piper did a one-eighty and ran. Leo was right behind them.

He expected to hear screaming from the Maenads. Instead, he heard laughter. He glanced back and saw the Maenads dancing through the flames in their bare feet. Their dresses were smoldering, but the Maenads didn't seem to care. They leaped through the fire like they were playing in a sprinkler.

"Thank you, unbeliever!" Babette laughed. "Our frenzy makes us immune to fire, but it does tickle! Trixie, send the unbelievers a thank-you gift!"

Trixie skipped over to the pile of boulders. She grasped a rock the size of a refrigerator and lifted it over her head.

"Run!" Piper said.

"We *are* running!" Jason picked up the speed.

"Run better!" Leo shouted.

They reached the edge of the clearing when a shadow passed overhead.

"Veer left!" Leo yelled.

They dove into the trees as the boulder slammed next to them with a jaw-rattling *thud*, missing Leo by a few inches. They skidded down a ravine until Leo lost his footing. He plowed into Jason and Piper so they ended up rolling downhill like a demigod snowball. They crashed into Brooke's stream at the bottom, helped each other up, and stumbled deeper into the woods. Behind them, Leo heard the Maenads laughing and shouting, urging Leo to come back so they could rip him to shreds.

For some reason, Leo wasn't tempted.

Jason pulled them behind a massive oak tree, where they stood gasping for breath. Piper's elbow was scraped up pretty badly. Jason's left pants leg had ripped almost completely off, so it looked like his leg was wearing a denim cape. Somehow, they'd all made it down the hill without killing themselves with their own weapons, which was a miracle.

"How do we beat them?" Jason demanded. "They're immune to fire. They're superstrong."

"We can't kill them," Piper said.

"There has to be a way," Leo said.

"No. We *can't* kill them," Piper said. "Anyone who kills a Maenad is cursed by Dionysus. Haven't you read the old stories? People who kill his followers go crazy or get morphed into animals or . . . well, bad stuff."

"Worse than letting the Maenads rip us to shreds?" Jason asked.

Piper didn't answer. Her face was so clammy, Leo decided not to ask for details.

"That's just great," Jason said. "So we have to stop them without killing them. Anyone got a really big piece of flypaper?"

"We're outnumbered four to one," Piper said. "Plus . . ." She grabbed Leo's wrist and checked his watch. "We have twenty minutes until Bunker Nine explodes."

"It's impossible," Jason summed up.

"We're dead," Piper agreed.

But Leo's mind was spinning into overdrive. He did his best work when things were impossible.

Stopping the Maenads without killing them . . . Bunker 9 . . . *flypaper*. An idea came together like one of his crazy contraptions, all the gears and pistons clicking into place perfectly.

"I've got it," he said. "Jason, you'll have to find Buford. You know which way he went. Circle back and find him, then bring him to the bunker, quick! Once you're far enough from the Maenads, maybe you can control the winds again. Then you can fly."

Jason frowned. "What about you two?"

"We're going to lead the Maenads out of your way," Leo said, "straight to Bunker Nine."

Piper coughed. "Excuse me, but isn't Bunker Nine about to *explode*?"

"Yes, but if I can get the Maenads inside, I have a way to take care of them."

Jason looked skeptical. "Even if you can, I'll still have to find Buford and get the syncopator back to you in twenty minutes, or you, Piper, and a dozen crazy nymphs will blow up."

"Trust me," Leo said. "And it's nineteen minutes now."

"I love this plan." Piper leaned over and kissed Jason. "In case I explode. Please hurry."

Jason didn't even respond. He bolted into the woods.

"Come on," Leo told Piper. "Let's invite the Maenads over to my place."

———·———

Leo had played games in the woods before—mostly capture-the-flag—but even Camp Half-Blood's full combat version wasn't nearly as dangerous as running from Maenads. Piper and he retraced their steps in the fading sunlight. Their breath steamed. Occasionally Leo would shout, "Party over here!" to let the Maenads know where they were. It was tricky, because Leo had to stay far enough ahead to avoid getting caught, but close enough so the Maenads wouldn't lose their trail.

Occasionally he heard startled cries as the Maenads happened across some unfortunate monster or nature spirit. Once a blood-chilling shriek pierced the air, followed by a sound like a tree getting destroyed by an army of savage chipmunks. Leo was so scared that he could hardly keep his feet moving. He figured some poor dryad had just gotten her life source shredded to splinters. Leo knew nature spirits got reincarnated, but that death cry was still the most awful thing he'd ever heard.

"Unbelievers!" Babette shouted through the woods. "Come celebrate with us!"

She sounded much closer now. Leo's instincts told him to just keep running. Forget Bunker 9. Maybe he and Piper could make it to the edge of the blast zone.

And then what . . . leave Jason to die? Let the Maenads blow up so Leo could suffer the curse of Dionysus? And would the explosion even *kill* Maenads? Leo had no idea. What if the Maenads survived and kept searching for Dionysus? Eventually they'd stumbled across the cabins and the other campers. No, that wasn't an option. Leo had to protect his friends. He could still save the *Argo II*.

"Over here!" he yelled. "Party at my house!"

He grabbed Piper's wrist and sprinted for the bunker.

He could hear the Maenads closing fast—bare feet running across the grass, branches snapping, eggnog goblets shattering against rocks.

"Almost there." Piper pointed through the woods. A hundred yards ahead rose a sheer limestone cliff that marked the entrance to Bunker 9.

Leo's heart felt like a combustion chamber going critical, but they made it to the cliff. He slapped his hand against the limestone. Fiery lines burned across the cliff face, slowly forming the outline of a massive door.

"Come on! Come on!" Leo urged.

He made the mistake of glancing back. Only a stone's throw away, the first Maenad appeared out of the woods. Her eyes were pure red. She grinned with a mouth full of fangs, then slashed her talon fingernails at the nearest tree and sliced it in half. Little tornadoes of leaves swirled around her as if even the air were going crazy.

"Come, demigod!" she called. "Join me in the revels!"

Leo knew it was insane, but her words buzzed in his ears. Part of him wanted to run toward her.

Whoa, boy, he told himself. *Golden Rule for Demigods: Thou shalt not Hokey Pokey with psychos.*

Still, he took a step toward the Maenad.

"Stop, Leo." Piper's charmspeak saved him, freezing him in place. "It's the madness of Dionysus affecting you. You *don't* want to die."

He took a shaky breath. "Yeah. They're getting stronger. We've got to hurry."

Finally the bunker doors opened. The Maenad snarled. Her friends emerged from the woods, and together they charged.

"Turn around!" Piper called to them in her most persuasive voice. "We're fifty yards behind you!"

It was a ridiculous suggestion, but the charmspeak momentarily worked. The Maenads turned and ran back the way they'd come, then stumbled to a halt, looking confused.

Leo and Piper ducked inside the bunker.

"Close the door?" Piper asked.

"No!" Leo said. "We want them inside."

"We *do*? What's the plan?"

"Plan." Leo tried to shake the fogginess from his brain.

They had thirty seconds, tops, before the Maenads poured in.

The *Argo II*'s engine would explode in—he checked his watch—oh, gods, twelve minutes?

"What can I do?" Piper asked. "Come on, Leo."

His mind began to clear. This was *his* territory. He couldn't let the Maenads win.

From the nearest worktable, Leo snatched a bronze control box with a single red button. He handed it to Piper. "I need two minutes. Climb the catwalks. Distract the Maenads like you did outside, okay? When I shout the order, wherever you are, push that button. But *not* before I say."

"What does it do?" Piper asked.

"Nothing yet. I have to set the trap."

"Two minutes." Piper nodded grimly. "You got it."

She ran to the nearest ladder and began to climb while Leo raced off down the aisles, snatching things from tool chests and supply cabinets. He grabbed machine parts and wires. He threw switches and activated time-delay sensors on the bunker's interior control panels. He didn't think about what he was doing any more than a pianist thinks about where his fingers are landing on the keyboard. He just flew through the bunker, bringing all the pieces of together.

He heard the Maenads rushing into the bunker. For a moment, they stopped in amazement, oohing and ahhing at the vast cavern full of shiny stuff.

"Where are you?" Babette called. "My fake lord Dionysus! Party with us!"

Leo tried to shut out her voice. Then he heard Piper, somewhere in the catwalks above, call out: "How about we square dance? Turn to the left!"

The Maenads shrieked in confusion.

"Grab a partner!" Piper shouted. "Swing her around!"

More cries and shrieking and a few *CLANGS* as some of the Maenads apparently swung each other into heavy metal objects.

"Stop it!" Babette yelled. "Do not grab a partner! Grab that demigod!"

Piper shouted a few more commands, but she seemed to be losing her sway.

Leo heard feet banging on the rungs of ladders.

"Oh, Leo?" Piper yelled. "Has it been two minutes?"

"Just a sec!" Leo found the last thing he needed—a quilt-sized stack of shimmering golden fabric. He fed the metallic cloth into the nearest pneumatic tube and pulled the lever. Done—assuming the plan worked.

He ran to the middle of the bunker, right in front of the *Argo II*, and yelled, "Hey! Here I am!"

He held out his arms and grinned. "Come on! Party with me!"

He glanced at the counter on the ship's engine. Six and a half minutes left. He wished he hadn't looked.

The Maenads climbed down from the ladders and began circling him warily. Leo danced and sang random television theme songs, hoping it would make them hesitate. He needed all the Maenads together before he sprung the trap.

"Sing along!" he said.

The Maenads snarled. Their blood-red eyes looked angry and annoyed. Their wreaths of snakes hissed. Their thyrsus rods glowed with purple fire.

Babette was the last to join the party. When she saw Leo alone, unarmed and dancing, she laughed with delight.

"You are wise to accept your fate," she said. "The *real* Dionysus would be pleased."

"Yeah, about that," Leo said. "I think there's a reason he changed his number. You guys aren't followers. You're crazy rabid stalkers. You haven't found him because he doesn't *want* you to."

"Lies!" Babette said. "We are the spirits of the wine god! He is proud of us!"

"Sure," Leo said. "I've got some crazy relatives too. I don't blame Mr. D."

"Kill him!" Babette shrieked.

"Wait!" Leo held up his hands. "You can kill me, but you want this to be a *real* party, don't you?"

As he'd hoped, the Maenads wavered.

"Party?" asked Candy.

"Party?" asked Buffy.

"Oh, yeah!" Leo looked up and shouted to the catwalks: "Piper? It's time to crank things up!"

For three incredibly long seconds, nothing happened. Leo just stood there grinning at a dozen frenzied nymphs who wanted to dice him into bite-sized demigod cubes.

Then the whole bunker whirred to life. All around the Maenads, pipes rose from the floor and blew purple steam. The pneumatic tube system spit out metal shavings like glittered confetti. The magic banner above them shimmered and changed to read WELCOME, PSYCHO NYMPHS!

Music blared from the sound system—the Rolling Stones, Leo's mom's favorite band. He liked to listen to them while he worked, because it reminded him of the good old days when he hung out in his mom's shop.

Then the winch system swung into place, and a mirrored ball began to descend right over Leo's head.

On the catwalk above, Piper stared down at the chaos she'd wrought with the push of a button, and her jaw dropped. Even the Maenads looked impressed by Leo's instant party.

Given a few more minutes, Leo could've done much better— a laser show, pyrotechnics, maybe some appetizers and a drink machine. But for two minutes' work, it wasn't bad. A few Maenads began to square dance. One did the Hokey Pokey.

Only Babette looked unaffected. "What trick is this?" she demanded. "You do not party for Dionysus!"

"Oh, no?" Leo glanced up. The mirrored ball was almost within reach. "You haven't seen my final trick."

The ball opened up. A grappling hook dropped down, and Leo jumped for it.

"Get him!" Babette yelled. "Maenads, attack!"

Thankfully, she had trouble getting their attention. Piper started calling down square dancing instructions again, confusing them with odd commands. "Turn left, turn right, bonk your heads! Sit down, stand up, fall down dead!"

The pulley lifted Leo into the air as the Maenads swarmed underneath him, gathering in a nice compact cluster. Babette leaped at him. Her claws just missed his feet.

"Now!" he muttered to himself, praying that his timer was set accurately.

BLAM! The nearest pneumatic tube shot a curtain of golden mesh over the Maenads, covering them like a parachute. A perfect shot.

The Maenads struggled against the net. They tried pushing it off, cutting the ropes with their teeth and fingernails, but as they punched and kicked and struggled, the net simply changed shape, hardening into a cubical cage of glittered gold.

Leo grinned. "Piper, hit the button again!"

She did. The music died. The party ended.

Leo dropped from the hook onto the top of his newly made cage. He stomped on the roof, just to be sure, but it felt as hard as titanium.

"Let us out!" Babette shrieked. "What evil magic is this?"

She slammed against the woven bars, but even her superstrength was no match for the golden material. The other Maenads hissed and screamed and banged on the cage with their thyrsus rods.

Leo jumped to the ground. "This is *my* party now, ladies. That cage is made from Hephaestian netting, a little recipe my dad cooked up. Maybe you've heard the story. He caught his wife Aphrodite cheating on him with Ares, so Hephaestus threw a golden net over them and put them on display. They stayed trapped until my dad decided to let them out. That netting right there? That's made from the same stuff. If two gods couldn't escape it, you don't stand a chance."

Leo seriously hoped he was right about that. The furious Maenads raged around their prison, climbing over each other and trying to rip through the mesh with no success.

Piper slid down the ladder and joined him. "Leo, you are *amazing*."

"I know that." He looked at the digital display next to the ship's engine. His heart sank. "For about two more minutes. Then I stop being amazing."

"Oh, no." Piper's face fell. "We need to get out of here!"

Suddenly Leo heard a familiar sound from the bunker entrance: a puff of steam, the creak of gears, and the *clink-clank* of metal legs running across the floor.

"Buford!" Leo called. The automated table chuffed toward him, whirring and clacking its drawers.

Jason walked in behind him, grinning. "Waiting for us?"

Leo hugged the little worktable. "I'm so sorry, Buford. I promise I'll never take you for granted again. *Only* Lemon Pledge with extra-moisturizing formula, my friend. Anytime you want it!"

Buford puffed steam happily.

"Um, Leo?" Piper urged. "The explosion?"

"Right!" Leo opened Buford's front drawer and grabbed the syncopator. He ran to the combustion chamber. Twenty-three seconds. Oh, good. No rush.

He would only get one chance to do this right. Leo carefully fitted the syncopator into place. He closed the combustion chamber and held his breath. The engine started to hum. The glass cylinders glowed with heat. If Leo hadn't been immune to fire, he was pretty sure he would have gotten a nasty sunburn.

The ship's hull shuddered. The whole bunker seemed to tremble.

"Leo?" Jason asked tightly.

"Hold on," Leo said.

"Let us out!" Babette screeched in her golden cage. "If you destroy us, Dionysus will make you suffer!"

"He'll probably send us a thank-you card," Piper grumbled. "But it won't matter. We'll all be dead."

The combustion chamber opened its various chambers with a *click, click, click.* Superdangerous liquids and gases flowed into the syncopator. The engine shuddered. Then the heat subsided, and the shaking calmed down to a comfortable purr.

Leo put his hand on the hull, now thrumming with the magical energy. Buford snuggled affectionately against his leg and puffed steam.

"That's right, Buford." Leo turned proudly to his friends. "That is the sound of an engine *not* exploding."

———

Leo didn't realize how stressed he'd been until he passed out.

When he woke up, he was lying on a cot near the *Argo II.* The entire Hephaestus cabin was there. They'd gotten the engine levels stabilized and were all expressing their amazement at Leo's genius.

Once he was back on his feet, Jason and Piper pulled him aside and promised they hadn't told anyone just how close the ship had come to exploding. No one would ever know about the huge mistake that almost vaporized the woods.

Still, Leo couldn't stop trembling. He'd almost ruined everything. To calm himself down, he pulled out the Lemon Pledge and carefully polished Buford. Then he took the spare syncopator and locked it in a supply cabinet that did *not* have legs. Just in case. Buford could be temperamental.

An hour later, Chiron and Argus arrived from the Big House to take care of the Maenads.

Argus, the head of security, was a big blond dude with hundreds of eyes all over his body. He seemed embarrassed to find that a dozen dangerous Maenads had infiltrated his territory unnoticed. Argus never spoke, but he blushed brightly and all the eyes on his body stared at the floor.

Chiron, the camp director, looked more annoyed than concerned. He stared down at the Maenads—which he could do, being a centaur. From the waist down, he was white stallion. From the waist up, he was a middle-aged guy with curly brown hair, a beard, and a bow and quiver strapped across his back.

"Oh, them again," Chiron said. "Hello, Babette."

"We will destroy you!" Babette shrieked. "We will dance with you, feed you yummy appetizers, party with you until the wee hours, and rip you to pieces!"

"Uh-huh." Chiron looked unimpressed. He turned to Leo and his friends. "Well done, you three. The last time these girls came looking for Dionysus, they caused quite a nuisance. You caught them before they could get out of hand. Dionysus will be pleased they've been captured."

"So they *do* annoy him?" Leo asked.

"Absolutely," Chiron said. "Mr. D despises his fan club almost as much as he despises demigods."

"We are not a fan club!" Babette wailed. "We are his followers, his chosen, his special ones!"

"Uh-huh," Chiron said again.

"So . . ." Piper shifted uneasily. "Dionysus wouldn't have minded if we had to destroy them?"

"Oh, no, he would mind!" Chiron said. "They're still his followers, even if he hates them. If you hurt them, Dionysus would be forced to drive you insane or kill you. Probably both. So well done." He looked at Argus. "Same plan as last time?"

Argus nodded. He gestured to one of the Hephaestus campers, who drove a forklift over and loaded up the cage.

"What will you do with them?" Jason asked.

Chiron smiled kindly. "We'll send them to a place where they feel at home. We'll load them on a bus to Atlantic City."

"Ouch," Leo said. "Doesn't that place have enough problems?"

"Not to worry," Chiron promised. "The Maenads will get the partying out of their systems very quickly. They'll wear themselves out and fade away until next year. They always seem to show up around the holidays. Quite annoying."

The Maenads were carted off. Chiron and Argus headed back to the Big House, and Leo's campers helped him lock up Bunker 9 for the night.

Usually Leo worked into the wee hours, but he decided he'd done enough for one day. It was Christmas Eve, after all. He'd earned a break.

Camp Half-Blood didn't really celebrate mortal holidays, but everyone was in a good mood at the campfire. Some kids were drinking eggnog. Leo, Jason, and Piper passed on that and went for hot chocolate instead.

They listened to sing-along songs and watched sparks from the fire curl up toward the stars.

"You saved my hide again, guys," Leo told his friends. "Thank you."

Jason smiled. "Anything for you, Valdez. You sure the *Argo II* will be safe now?"

"Safe? No. But she's not in danger of exploding. Probably."

Piper laughed. "Great. I feel much better."

They sat quietly, enjoying each other's company, but Leo knew this was just a brief moment of peace. The *Argo II* had to be finished by the summer solstice. Then they would sail off on their great adventure—first to find Jason's old home, the Roman camp. After that . . . the giants were waiting. Gaea the earth mother, the most powerful enemy of the gods, was marshaling her forces to destroy Olympus. To stop her, Leo and his friends would have to sail to Greece, the ancient homeland of the gods. At any point along the way, Leo knew he might die.

For now, though, he decided to enjoy himself. When your life is on a timer to an inevitable explosion, that's about all you can do.

He raised his goblet of hot chocolate. "To friends."

"Friends," Piper and Jason agreed.

Leo stayed at the campfire until the song leader from Apollo cabin suggested they all do the Hokey Pokey. Then Leo decided to call it a night.

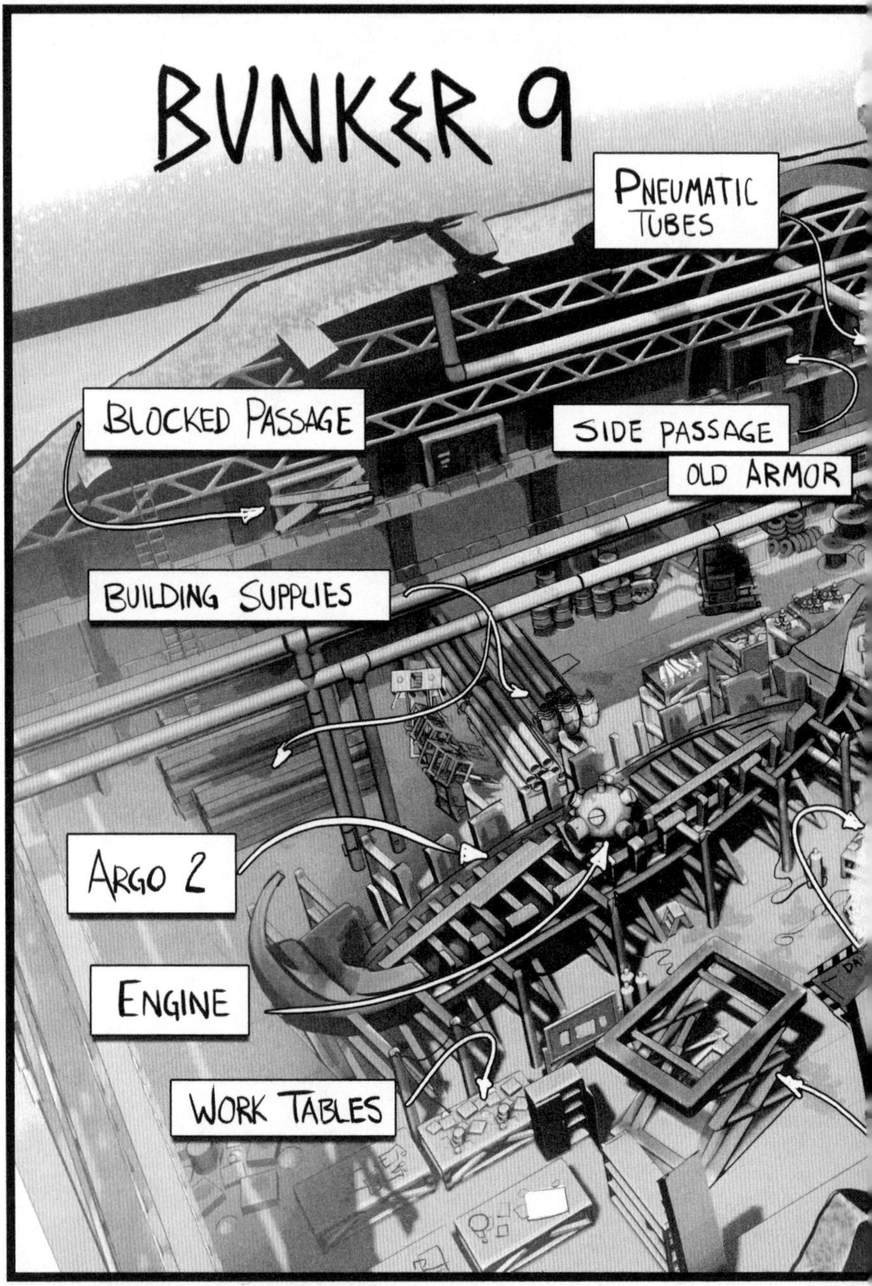

BUNKER 9
PNEUMATIC TUBES
BLOCKED PASSAGE
SIDE PASSAGE
OLD ARMOR
BUILDING SUPPLIES
ARGO 2
ENGINE
WORK TABLES

PROPHECY

SEVEN HALF-BLOODS

SHALL ANSWER THE CALL.

TO STORM OR FIRE,

THE WORLD MUST FALL.

AN OATH TO KEEP WITH A FINAL BREATH,

AND FOES BEAR ARMS

TO THE DOORS OF DEATH.

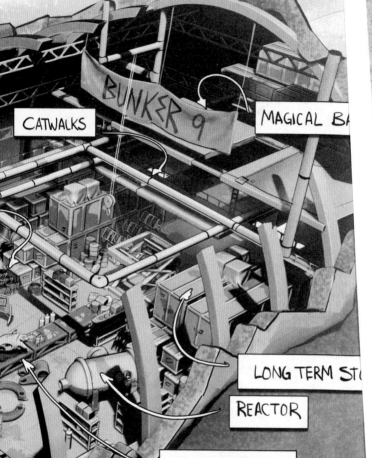

CATWALKS

BUNKER 9

MAGICAL BA

LONG TERM STO

REACTOR

ARGO MASTHEAD

SKETCHBOOKS MAPS & BLUEPRINTS

HYDRAULIC LIFT

WORD SCRAMBLE

Unscramble the words below to find out which
seven half-bloods must band together
to fulfill the prophecy's quest!
(answer key on page 176)

SNOJA _ _ _ _ _

ELO _ _ _

IEPRP _ _ _ _ _

FANKR _ _ _ _ _

ZLAHE _ _ _ _ _

ERYPC _ _ _ _ _

NHNETABA _ _ _ _ _ _ _ _

OLYMPIAN WORD SEARCH

Discover the hidden words lurking in this puzzle!
(answer key on page 177)

```
N  P  E  R  C  Y  M  D  E  D  E  A  S  W  P  W
M  A  E  N  A  D  G  I  O  S  A  B  N  A  I  L
F  N  A  U  P  I  I  O  J  N  E  G  L  R  P  P
R  N  T  V  B  Q  L  E  O  Q  A  Z  G  E  E  P
A  A  E  U  U  B  H  C  W  I  A  G  O  E  R  L
H  B  S  R  F  T  U  O  L  I  E  E  I  O  R  E
P  E  R  L  O  C  V  A  W  K  P  G  G  D  E  U
V  T  A  R  R  T  H  Q  U  L  A  R  T  I  L  C
R  H  M  O  D  T  A  L  I  I  A  U  E  A  S  R
N  I  A  H  M  Y  L  N  P  Z  N  N  I  R  T  O
C  A  L  G  C  H  C  U  P  C  O  T  Q  Y  F  T
G  O  T  I  F  H  Y  U  I  U  O  T  E  Y  K  A
I  G  H  R  L  E  O  F  K  S  J  A  S  O  N  E
R  L  E  U  C  R  N  T  A  E  A  A  N  N  D  O
E  P  I  R  L  M  A  J  L  O  I  C  A  C  U  S
S  N  A  T  H  E  F  E  S  T  U  S  D  S  E  R
T  O  P  Z  E  S  C  E  L  E  S  T  I  A  L  H
```

174

AEGIS	DAGGER	LEO
AMALTHEIA	DIARY	LEUCROTAE
ANNABETH	FESTUS	LUKE
ARGO	HALCYON	MAENAD
BUFORD	HALF BLOOD	PERCY
CACUS	HERMES	PIPER
CELESTIAL	JASON	THALIA

Answer Key

Word Scramble Answers

Jason, Leo, Piper, Frank,
Hazel, Percy, and Annabeth
must unite to answer
the prophecy's call

OLYMPIAN WORD SEARCH ANSWERS

N	P	E	R	C	Y	M	D	E	D	E	A	S	W	P	W
M	A	E	N	A	D	G	I	O	S	A	B	N	A	I	L
F	N	A	U	P	I	I	O	J	N	E	G	L	R	P	P
R	N	T	V	B	Q	L	E	O	Q	A	Z	G	E	E	P
A	A	E	U	U	B	H	C	W	I	A	G	O	E	R	L
H	B	S	R	F	T	U	O	L	I	E	E	I	O	R	E
P	E	R	L	O	C	V	A	W	K	P	G	G	D	E	U
V	T	A	R	R	T	H	Q	U	L	A	R	T	I	L	C
R	H	M	O	D	T	A	L	I	I	A	U	E	A	S	R
N	I	A	H	M	Y	L	N	P	Z	N	N	I	R	T	O
C	A	L	G	C	H	C	U	P	C	O	T	Q	Y	F	T
G	O	T	I	F	H	Y	U	I	U	O	T	E	Y	K	A
I	G	H	R	L	E	O	F	K	S	J	A	S	O	N	E
R	L	E	U	C	R	N	T	A	E	A	A	N	N	D	O
E	P	I	R	L	M	A	J	L	O	I	C	A	C	U	S
S	N	A	T	H	E	F	E	S	T	U	S	D	S	E	R
T	O	P	Z	E	S	C	E	L	E	S	T	I	A	L	H

177

A Note from
RICK RIORDAN

PERCY JACKSON began as a bedtime story for my son Haley. In the spring of 2002, when Haley was in first grade, he began having trouble at school. We soon found out he had ADHD and dyslexia. This made reading difficult for him, but he *did* enjoy Greek mythology, which I had taught in middle school for many years. To keep him interested in reading, I began telling Haley myths at home. When I ran out, he asked me to make up a new one. The result was Percy Jackson, the modern ADHD/dyslexic demigod, inspired by my son's own struggle.

Over the years, Haley and Percy have grown up together. Percy became a hero. Haley did some pretty heroic things too. He learned to overcome his learning disabilities, excelled in school, became a voracious reader, and—much to my astonishment—decided he wanted to write books of his own. He recently completed his first manuscript for a novel, which is longer than anything I've ever written! I also have to admit his writing skills are light-years beyond where mine were at age sixteen.

At the time of this writing, Haley and Percy are the same

age—sixteen. It's amazing to me how far both of them have come. When I was planning this book of stories, it occurred to me that Haley might have something to say about Percy's world. After all, he inspired it. If not for his encouragement, I never would've written down *The Lightning Thief.*

I asked Haley if he'd like to contribute a story for *Demigod Diaries*. He immediately took up the challenge. The result is "Son of Magic," in which Haley carves out new territory in Percy's world. His story hinges on an intriguing question: After *The Last Olympian*, what happened to the demigods who fought in Kronos's army?

You're about to meet one of those demigods. You're also going to get some answers about how the Mist works, and why monsters can "smell" heroes. I wish I'd come up with these ideas!

It seems only fitting that Haley and I have come full circle. The boy who inspired me to create Percy Jackson is now writing about Percy's world himself. It's my pleasure to introduce "Son of Magic," the debut story from Haley Riordan.

SON

OF

MAGIC

BY

HALEY RIORDAN

"NORMALLY I INVITE PEOPLE to ask me questions when I'm finished, but this time I have one I'd like to ask you all instead." He took a step back, trying to make eye contact with each and every one of the thousand audience members. "When you die, what happens? The question seems so childish, doesn't it? But do any of you know the answer?"

There was silence, just like there was supposed to be. . . .

Dr. Claymore didn't expect anyone to answer the question after the speech he'd just given. He didn't think anyone would even dare to try.

But as always, someone dashed his hopes.

This time it was the brown-haired, freckle-faced boy in the front of the auditorium. Claymore recognized him—it was the same kid who had run up to him in the parking lot, telling him what a big fan he was and how he'd read all his books. . . .

"Yes?" Dr. Claymore asked him. "You think you know? Then please, we are all *dying* to hear you."

The boy who had been so energetic before now seemed tongue-tied.

Claymore knew it was cruel to make a fool out of this innocent child. But he also knew it was necessary.

Claymore was just an actor, performing for his patrons like any good showman would during a magic show. And this boy had just volunteered to be part of his act.

At this point the entire audience was staring at the child. The man sitting next to him—the boy's father, Claymore assumed— shifted uncomfortably in his seat.

With so much attention focused on him, Claymore doubted the child would even have the strength to breathe. He looked so frail—skinny and awkward, probably the butt of many a joke at his school.

But then the seemingly weak boy did something surprising. He stood up and found his voice.

"We don't know," the boy said. His entire body was shaking, but he met Claymore's gaze. "You criticize every single idea people have about the afterlife. After all your research, why are you asking us for an answer? Haven't you found one yourself?"

Claymore didn't respond immediately. Had the boy said "heaven" or "reincarnation," he would have snapped back like a whip, but these comments were different. They made his act come to a screeching halt. The audience turned their eyes on him

with a berating gaze, as if they found it easier to cling to the boy's
simplistic words than to Claymore's life's work.

But like any good showman, Claymore had a backup plan. He
didn't let more than five seconds pass. Any longer, and he would
have seemed nervous. Any shorter, and it would seem like he was
lashing out. After the appropriate pause, he gave his rehearsed
response.

"I'm asking all of you because I am still searching for the answer
myself," he said, gripping the podium. "And the most complicated
truths sometimes come from the simplest places. When I am on
my deathbed, I want to know with unwavering certainty what lies
ahead of me. I'm sure each and every one of you feels the same
way."

The audience applauded. Claymore waited for them to finish.

"My new book, *Road to Death*, will be in stores soon," he con-
cluded. "If you want to know more, I'd be honored to have you read
it. And now I wish you good night. I hope you all find the answers
you seek."

A few in the audience gave him a standing ovation. Claymore
flashed one last smile before walking offstage. But once he was
away from their eyes, he scowled.

This was what his life had come to—being paraded around
from one event to another like some circus animal. He was a
visionary, but at the same time, a joke. Maybe a dozen people in

the audience even remotely understood his work. He knew even fewer would accept it.

The sheer ignorance of his fans disgusted him.

"Mr. Claymore!" His host trotted backstage, and Claymore bent his frown into a smile. She was the one paying his fee, after all.

"You were a hit, Mr. Claymore!" she said, nearly jumping out of her high heels. "We've never had such a crowd!"

The woman landed back on her feet, and Claymore was surprised that her heels didn't shatter under her weight. That was probably an impolite thought, but this woman almost matched him in height, and Claymore was considered a tall person. The best way to describe her would be as a stereotypical grandmother, the kind who bakes cookies and knits sweaters. She was larger than most grandmas, however. And her enthusiasm was fierce, almost like a hunger. A hunger for what? he wondered. Claymore assumed more cookies.

"Thank you," he said, gritting his teeth. "But it's *Doctor* Claymore, actually."

"Well, you were amazing!" she said, smiling ear to ear. "You're the first author we've sold out for!"

Of course I would fill the auditorium in a tiny town like this, Claymore thought. More than one reviewer had called him the greatest mind since Stephen Hawking. Even as a child, he'd used his silver tongue to make him seem little less than a god to his peers and teachers. Now he was looked up to by politicians and scientists alike.

"I preach the truth, and people long for the truth about death," he said, quoting his new book.

The woman seemed a bit starstruck and no doubt would have kept praising him for hours, but she had served her purpose; so Claymore used the opportunity to make his departure. "I need to retire to my home now, Ms. Lamia. Have a good night."

With those words, he walked out of the building and into the crisp night air.

He never would have agreed to speak in backwater Keeseville, New York, if he didn't own a home here. The massive auditorium stuck out like a sore thumb in this quaint little town where he'd moved to pursue his writing in peace.

With its population barely breaking two thousand, Claymore guessed that the huge crowd tonight must have come from all over the state. He was a special event, a once-in-a-lifetime thing. But for Claymore it was busywork, something his publishers required of him. Just another day at the office.

"Dr. Claymore, wait!" a voice called after him, but he ignored it.

If it wasn't his sponsor, he didn't have to answer. There was no point . . . the event was over. But then someone grabbed his arm.

He turned and glared. It was *that* boy, the same one who had tried to make a fool of him.

"Dr. Claymore!" the boy said, panting. "Hold on. I need to ask you something."

Claymore opened his mouth to reprimand the child, but then he stopped.

The boy's father stood a few feet behind him. At least, Claymore assumed it was the father. They shared the same brown hair and lanky physique.

He thought the man should scold his child for being so rude, but the father just stared blankly at Claymore.

"Why, yes, hello," Claymore said, forcing a smile toward the dad. "Is this your son?"

"He just has a quick question for you," the dad said absent-mindedly.

Claymore reluctantly turned his gaze to the boy, who, unlike his father, had eyes burning with fiery determination.

"I suppose this is my fault," Claymore said as civilly as possible. "I should have allowed you more time to talk at the end of my speech."

"It's something important," the boy said. "So please take this seriously even if it sounds weird, okay?"

Claymore resisted the urge to walk away. He disliked indulging people, but his public face was important to his book sales. He couldn't have this boy's idiot father telling the world that they had been cruelly ignored.

"Ask away," Claymore said. "I'm all ears."

The boy straightened. Despite being as thin as a twig, he stood nearly as tall as Claymore.

"What happens if someone finds a way to stop death?"

Claymore could feel his blood chill from the change in the boy's voice. It wasn't nervous anymore. It was as heavy and cold as stone.

"That would be impossible," Claymore said. "All living things decay over time. There is a certain point at which we become unable to function. That is—"

"You didn't answer the question," the boy interrupted. "Please give me your honest opinion."

"I don't have one," Claymore retorted. "I'm not a fiction writer. I don't indulge myself in impossibilities."

The boy frowned. "That's too bad. Dad, the paper?"

The man pulled a piece of paper from his pocket and handed it to Claymore.

"It's our contact information," the boy said. "If you figure it out, call me, okay?"

Claymore stared at him, trying not to let his confusion show. "You do understand me, don't you? I can't answer your question."

The boy looked at him with solemn eyes. "Please try, Dr. Claymore. Because if you don't, I'm going to die."

On the drive home Claymore kept glancing in his rearview mirror. Really, he was pathetic. The boy had just been trying to unnerve him. He couldn't let himself get upset over something like that.

By the time he reached his driveway, he felt like he had gotten over it. But he still found himself setting his house alarm.

Claymore lived alone in his personally designed house. Among his many talents he was an architect, and he wanted his house to mirror himself in every aspect. Impressively modern with clean lines, it was set well back from the road. Its security cameras and barred windows protected his privacy, but inside, the rooms were simply furnished, quiet, and comfortable.

No wife, no kids—there was no one in the house to disturb him. Not even a cat. *Especially* not a cat.

It was his oasis and *his* oasis alone. Being here always calmed his frayed nerves.

Yes, his beautiful house did help him get his mind off the boy. But it wasn't long before he found himself sitting at his desk, reading the card the father had given him.

ALABASTER C. TORRINGTON

273 MORROW LANE

518-555-9530

The 518 area code meant that they might live in Keeseville. And Claymore recalled a Morrow Lane about halfway across town.

Was Alabaster Torrington the boy, or the father? Alabaster was a rather old-fashioned name. You didn't hear it often, because most parents had the sense not to name their children after rocks.

Claymore shook his head. He should throw away the card and forget it. Scenes from Stephen King's *Misery* were stuck in his head. But that's what the alarm system is for, he told himself; to keep the creepy fans away. If his door got so much as a knock in the middle of the night, the police would be dispatched immediately.

And Claymore was not defenseless. He had a respectable collection of firearms hidden in various places around his house. One couldn't be too careful.

He sighed, throwing the piece of paper on the table with the rest of his scraps. It wasn't unusual for him to encounter strange people at events. After all, for every semi-intelligent person who bought his books, there were at least three others who picked them up because they thought they were dieting guides.

All that mattered was the fact that Claymore wasn't alone in a dark alley with those people. He was safe, he was home, and there was no better place to be.

He smiled to himself, leaning back in his work chair. "Yes, that's right, nothing to worry about," he told himself. "Just another day at the office."

That's when the phone rang, and Claymore's smile melted.

What could anyone want at this hour? It was nearly eleven. Anyone sensible was either asleep or curled up with a good book.

He thought about not answering, but his phone didn't stop ringing—which was very strange, considering that his voicemail usually picked up after the fourth ring. Eventually curiosity won him over.

He stood and walked into his great room. For simplicity's sake, he only kept one landline in the house. The caller ID read MARIAN LAMIA, 518-555-4164.

Lamia . . . That was the woman who booked the event.

He frowned and reluctantly picked up the receiver as he sat down on his couch.

"Yes, hello, Claymore speaking." He did not attempt to mask the annoyance in his voice. This was his home, and forcing him to answer a phone call was no better than intruding in person. He hoped Lamia had a good reason.

"Mr. Claymore!" She said his name like she was announcing he'd won the lottery. "Hello, hello, hello! How are you doing?"

"Do you realize what hour it is, Ms. Lamia?" Claymore asked in the most severe voice he could muster. "Do you have something important to tell me?"

"Yes, I do! In fact, I wanted to talk to you about it immediately!"

He sighed. This person made him go from mildly annoyed to just plain infuriated in a grand total of thirty seconds.

"Well, then, don't just exclaim pointlessly," he snarled. "Spit it out! I'm a busy man and do not take kindly to being disturbed."

The line went silent. Claymore was half convinced he'd scared her off. But finally she continued in a much colder voice.

"Very well, Mr. Claymore. We don't have to go through the pleasantries, if that's what you wish."

He nearly laughed. It sounded like this woman was outright *trying* to be intimidating.

"Thank you," Claymore said. "What exactly do you want?"

"You met a child tonight, and he gave you something," Lamia said. "I want you to hand that over to me."

He frowned. How did she know about the boy? Was she watching him?

"I don't appreciate your following me, but I guess at this point that hardly matters. All the child gave me was a piece of paper with his address on it. I wouldn't feel comfortable giving it to you, someone I met only yesterday."

There was another pause. Just as Claymore was about to put down the phone, the woman asked, "Do you believe in God, Mr. Claymore?"

He rolled his eyes, disgusted with the woman. "You don't know when to stop, do you? I don't believe in anything that I cannot see or feel myself. So if you are asking me from a religious context, the answer is no."

"That's a shame," she said, her voice barely a whisper. "It makes my job that much harder."

Claymore slammed down the receiver.

What was that woman's problem? She had started the conversation by practically saying, "I've been stalking you," and then tried to convert him. So much for her being a nice grandmother.

The phone rang again—Lamia's ID—but Claymore had absolutely no intention of picking it up. He unplugged his phone, and that was the end of that.

Tomorrow, perhaps, he'd file a police report. Clearly Ms. Lamia was deranged. Why on earth would she want that boy's address? What did Lamia want with him?

Claymore shivered. He felt a strange urge to warn the child. But no, this wasn't his problem. He would just let the psychos thin themselves out, if that's what they wished. He wasn't going to step into the crossfire.

Especially not tonight. Tonight, he needed to sleep.

———————

Claymore knew that curiosity and excitement could twist a person's dreams. But that didn't explain this one.

He found himself in a vast room, old and dusty. It looked like a church that hadn't been cleaned in a century. There was no light except for a soft green shimmer at the far end of room. The source of the light was obscured by a boy standing in the aisle directly in front him. Though Claymore couldn't see clearly, he was sure it was the same kid from the auditorium. What was *he* doing in Claymore's dream?

Claymore was what people called a lucid dreamer, someone who usually knows when they're dreaming and can wake up at will. He could have woken himself now if he'd wanted to, but he decided not to just yet. He was curious.

"She's found me again," the boy said. He wasn't addressing Claymore. His back was turned, and he seemed to be talking to the green light. "I don't know if I can fight her off this time. She's closing in on my scent."

For a moment there was no answer. Then, finally, a woman spoke from the front of the room. Her tone was stoic and without humor, and something about it sent a shiver up Claymore's spine.

"You know I cannot help you, my child," she said. "She is my daughter. I can't raise my hand against either of you."

The boy tensed like he was ready to argue, but he stopped himself. "I—I understand, Mother."

"Alabaster, you know I love you," the woman said. "But this is a battle you brought upon yourself. You accepted Kronos's blessing. You fought with his armies in my name. You can't simply turn to your enemies now and ask for forgiveness. They will never help you. I have bargained to keep you safe thus far, but I cannot interfere in your fight with *her*."

Claymore frowned. The name Kronos referred to the Titan

lord of Greek mythology, son of the earth and the heavens, but the rest made no sense. Claymore had hoped to gain some insight from this dream, but now it seemed like garbage—more mythology and legends. It was nothing but useless fiction.

The boy, Alabaster, stepped toward the green light. "Kronos wasn't supposed to lose! You said the odds of winning were in the Titans' favor! You told me Camp Half-Blood would be destroyed!"

When the boy moved, Claymore could finally see the woman that he was talking to. She knelt at the end of the aisle, her face raised as if in prayer to a dirty stained glass window above the altar. She was dressed in white robes covered with ornate silver designs, like runes or alchemy symbols. Her dark hair barely came down to her shoulders.

Despite the grime and dust she was kneeling in, the woman looked spotless. In fact *she* was the source of the light. The green shimmer surrounded her like an aura.

She spoke without looking at the boy. "Alabaster, I simply told you the most likely outcome. I didn't promise you that it would occur. I only wanted you see the options, so you would be prepared for what might lie ahead."

"All right," Claymore finally spoke up. "I've had enough. This ridiculous story ends now!"

He expected to snap back awake. But for some reason he didn't.

The boy wheeled around and examined him with amazement. *"You?"* He turned back to the kneeling woman. "Why is *he* here? Mortals aren't allowed to set foot in the house of a god!"

"He's here because I invited him in," the woman said. "You asked for his help, didn't you? I had hoped he would be more willing if he understood your—"

"Enough!" Claymore yelled. "This is absurd! This isn't reality! This is merely a dream, and as its creator, I demand to wake up!"

The woman still didn't look at him, but her voice sounded amused. "Very well, Dr. Claymore. If that is what you wish, I will make it so."

———

Claymore opened his eyes. Sunlight was streaming through his bedroom windows.

Odd . . . Usually when he chose to end a dream, he woke up immediately, during the dead of night. Why was it morning?

Well, if anything, that dream made the boy from yesterday seem a whole lot less intimidating. Kronos's blessing? The house of a god? Alabaster had sounded more like a member of a role-playing group than a crazed psycho. Titans? Claymore fought back a laugh. What was he, five?

Claymore felt relieved and refreshed. It was time to start his morning routine.

He slipped out of his bedclothes, showered, and put on his regular attire—the same style of clothes he'd worn to his speech the night before: slacks, dress shirt, polished brown loafers. Claymore did not believe in dressing down.

He slipped on his tweed jacket and started to gather his belongings.

Laptop: check. Wallet: check. Keys: check.

Then he hesitated. There was one more thing he needed. It was a completely unnecessary precaution, but it would give him peace of mind. He opened his desk drawer, picked his smallest handgun—a nine-millimeter—and slipped it into his jacket pocket.

Last night the boy Alabaster had shaken him to his foundation. So much so that Claymore had gone to bed without doing any writing, which was not something he could afford right now, with his next deadline right around the corner. He could not allow any crazed fans to affect his mood and output. If that meant he had to carry a security blanket, then so be it.

———

Black's Coffee. The name was a pun of the worst kind, but still Claymore returned day after day. After all, it was the best coffee place in Keeseville. Then again, it was the *only* coffee place in Keeseville. . . .

He'd gotten to know the owner quite well. As soon as he

stepped inside, Burly Black was the first one to greet him with "Howard! How you doing? The usual?"

Burly was . . . well, burly. His beefy face, massive tattooed arms, and permanent scowl would have gained him entry into any biker gang. His *Kiss the Cook* apron was the only thing that made him look like he was supposed to be behind the counter.

"'Morning," Claymore replied, taking a seat at the counter and pulling out his laptop. "Yes, the usual is good."

He was on chapter forty-six at this point, which made his work easier. No more hand-holding the readers. If they hadn't gotten the point by now, they never would.

Coffee and a blueberry pastry appeared in front of him, but Claymore hardly noticed them. He was in his own world, fingers sprawling out on the keyboard, words and thoughts coming together in a seemingly incomprehensible pattern, but Claymore knew it was genius.

The coffee was slowly drained. The pastry was reduced to a few crumbs. Other customers came and went, but none of them fazed Claymore. Nothing mattered except his work. This was what he lived for.

But then his private world shattered when a woman sat down next to him.

"Claymore, what a surprise! I didn't expect to see you here!"

White-hot hatred welled up inside him. He hit control-S and

closed his laptop. "Ms. Lamia, if I were not a more civilized man, I'd pull that seat out from under you."

She pouted, giving him puppy eyes, which wasn't convincing in a woman her age. "That's not very nice, Mr. Claymore. I'm just saying hello."

He glared at her. "It's *Doctor* Claymore."

"I'm sorry," she said halfheartedly. "I always forget . . . I'm not very good with names, you see."

"The only thing I want from you is for you to leave my sight," he said. "I refuse to be converted to whatever cult you belong to."

"I just want to talk," she insisted. "It's not about gods. It's about the boy, Alabaster."

He eyed her suspiciously. How did she know the boy's name? Claymore hadn't mentioned it in their phone conversation last night.

Ms. Lamia smiled. "I've been looking for Alabaster for some time now. I'm his sister."

Claymore laughed. "Can't you make up a better lie than that? You're older than the boy's father!"

"Well, looks can be deceiving." Her eyes seemed unnaturally bright, luminous green, like the light in Claymore's dream. "The boy has concealed himself well," she continued. "I must admit he's gotten better at his *magia occultandi*. I hoped your speech would draw him into the open, and it did. But before I could grab him, he managed to escape. Give me his address, and I'll leave you in peace."

Claymore tried to stay calm. She was just a crazy old woman, rambling nonsense. Although *magia occultandi* . . . Claymore knew his Latin. That meant *enchantment of hiding*. Who in the world was this woman, and why did she want the boy? It was clear that she meant Alabaster harm.

As Claymore stared at her, he realized something else . . . Ms. Lamia wasn't blinking. Had he *ever* seen her blink?

"You know what? I'm sick and tired of this." Claymore's voice trembled in spite of himself. "Black, have you been listening?"

He looked across the counter at Burly. For some reason, Burly didn't respond. He just kept polishing coffee mugs.

"Oh, he can't hear you." Lamia's voice dropped to that same raspy whisper he'd heard last night on the phone. "We can control the Mist at will. He has no idea that I'm even here."

"Mist?" Claymore asked. "What on earth are you talking about? You must truly be insane!"

He stood, instinctively backing away, putting his hand on his coat pocket. "Burly, please kick this woman out before she completely spoils my morning!"

Burly still didn't respond. The big man stared right through Claymore as if he wasn't there.

Lamia gave him a cocky smile. "You know, Mr. Claymore, I

don't think I've ever encountered a mortal this arrogant before. Perhaps you need a demonstration."

"Don't you understand, Ms. Lamia? I don't have time for this! I will take my leave now, and as for . . ."

He didn't have time to finish. Lamia stood and her form began to shimmer. Her eyes were the first to change. Her irises expanded, glowing dark green. Her pupils narrowed into serpentine slits. She extended a hand and immediately her fingers shriveled and hardened, her nails turning into lizardlike claws.

"I can kill you right now, *Mr. Claymore*," she whispered.

Wait . . . No, that wasn't a whisper. It sounded more like a hiss.

Claymore pulled his gun from his jacket and pointed it at Lamia's head. He didn't understand what was happening—some sort of hallucinogen in his coffee, perhaps. But he couldn't let this woman—this *creature*—get the best of him.

Those talons could be an illusion, but she was still preparing to attack him.

"Do you really think I would act so cocky around a lunatic if I wasn't prepared to defend myself?" he asked.

She snarled and advanced, raising her claws.

Claymore had never shot anything before, but his instincts took over. He pulled the trigger. Lamia staggered, hissing.

"Life is a frail thing," he said. "Perhaps you should have read my books! I'm merely acting in self-defense!"

She lunged again. Claymore fired twice more at the woman's head, and she collapsed to the floor.

He'd expected there to be more blood . . . but it didn't matter. "You—you saw that, Burly, didn't you?" he demanded. "It couldn't be helped!"

He turned to Black, and then frowned. Burly was still polishing coffee cups.

There was no way for Burly not to have heard the gunshots. How was that possible? *How?*

And then yet another impossibility happened. The corpse below him started to move.

"I hope you understand now, Mr. Claymore." Lamia rose and stared at him with her one remaining serpent eye. The entire left side of her face had been blown off, but where blood and bone should have been there was a thick layer of black sand.

It looked more like Claymore had just destroyed part of a sandcastle . . . and even that part was slowly re-forming.

"By assaulting me with your mortal weapon," she hissed, "you have declared war on the children of Hecate! And I do not take war lightly!"

This . . . this wasn't a dream, drug-induced or otherwise. This was impossible. . . . How was this real? How was she still alive?

Focus! Claymore told himself. *Obviously it is real, since it just happened!*

And so, being a logical man, Claymore did the logical thing. He gripped his gun and ran.

———•———

The last time he'd seen a boot was years ago, on a rental car he'd illegally parked in Manhattan—but now, of course, on this morning of all mornings, there was one on his car tire. Driving away was no longer an option.

Lamia was getting closer. She shuffled out of the café, her left eye slowing regenerating into an angry stare.

A car drove by and Claymore tried to wave it down, but just as had happened with Black, the driver didn't seem to register him.

"Don't you understand?" Lamia hissed. "Your mortal brethren can't see you! You're in my world!"

Claymore didn't argue. He took her explanation for it.

She wobbled toward him, taking her time. She seemed less like a serpent now, and more like a cat toying with its prey.

There was no way he could fight her off, either. He only had five shots left. If three bullets to the head wouldn't stop her, he doubted that anything short of a hand grenade would.

He had one advantage. He wasn't an athlete by any stretch of the imagination, but Lamia looked like she would have a hard time getting from her couch to the fridge. He could run and outlast her, no matter what kind of monster she was.

She was about ten feet away now. Claymore gave her a defiant smirk, then turned and sprinted down Main Street. There were only a dozen shops in the center of town, and the street was too open. He'd have turn on Second Avenue, possibly lose her on one of the side streets. Then he'd return to his home, trip his security, and get in touch with the police. Once he was there, he'd . . .

"*Incantare: Gelu Semita!*" Lamia screamed behind him.

That was Latin . . . an incantation. She was reciting some sort of spell.

He didn't have time to translate the phrase before the air around him seemed to drop thirty degrees. Even though there wasn't a cloud in the sky, hail started to fall. He turned, but Lamia was gone.

"*Incantation: Path of Frost . . .*" he translated aloud, his breath steaming. "Really? She's using magic? This is ridiculous!"

Then her voice spoke behind him: "You truly are an intelligent man, Mr. Claymore. Now I understand why my brother seeks you."

He spun toward her voice, but again she wasn't there.

Playing more games with him . . . Fine. He would have to do more than just run away. She wasn't human, but he would approach her like any adversary. He would have to study his opponent, learn her weaknesses.

And then he would make his escape.

He held his hand out to the hail. "I might not have known

this was possible ten minutes ago, but I understand one thing: If this is the extent of your power, it's no wonder we don't see more monsters like you!" He grinned. "We must have killed them all!"

She hissed in fury. The hail started coming down harder, filling the air with icy mist. He held out his gun, ready for her to come at him from any angle.

Even though he didn't care for fiction, he'd spent his career researching ancient beliefs. Incantations were actually a simple concept: if you say something with enough power behind it, it can come true.

This incantation had to be a translocational spell of some sort. Otherwise she wouldn't have used the word *semita*. She was making a path for herself, and this ice was the method of travel— obscuring her location and making it hard for Claymore to move or anticipate her next attack.

It was meant to unnerve him, but he forced himself to focus. The ground around him was now covered with ice. He stayed still and listened. He knew she would use the opportunity to strike.

She may have been toying with him, but Claymore had no intention of dying at the hands of an idiot like her, especially if she fell for his taunt so easily. . . .

Claymore heard the telltale sound of her high heels crunching against the ice. He whirled immediately, sidestepping as she raked her claws at the spot where he'd been standing. Before she could get back her balance, he fired.

Her left kneecap exploded into black dust, and the hail died down. Lamia stumbled, though by the look on her face, the wound didn't even faze her.

The lower half of her leg had disintegrated, but it was already re-forming.

He hadn't expected to kill her this time. He watched carefully as she healed, timing her regeneration. With one bullet, he estimated he'd bought himself a minute of time.

"You still don't understand, mortal!" she said. "Those weapons can't kill me! They can only slow me down!"

Claymore looked at her and laughed. "If you think I'm trying to kill you, you must really be daft! Obviously, I know you're immortal now, so why would I even try? No, I can't kill you. But I have gleaned something interesting from our time together." He aimed his gun. "You don't want to kill me right away. Otherwise you wouldn't have wasted your time pelting me with ice cubes. You want to scare me, hoping I'll lead you to the boy. He's a threat to you, isn't he? All I have to do is find him so he can dispose of you properly. And I know exactly where he is!"

She hissed as her leg reattached, but he shot off her other one.

"If I had enough bullets I could sit here all day!" Claymore jeered. "You're helpless! Maybe I should just get a vacuum and be done with you!"

He thought that the beast would realize she was at his mercy by now, but for some reason, she still smiled.

The hail had completely died down. What was on the ground had already melted back into nothingness, so he knew whatever spell she was using was over. How did she still have the audacity to smile?

"You really are the most arrogant mortal I've ever seen! Fine! If you won't lead me to the boy, I'll take pleasure in destroying you!" She flicked a serpentlike tongue. *"Incantare: Templum Incendere!"*

"Temple of Fire," Claymore translated.

Probably an offensive spell—he was about to be attacked by fire somehow. He shot her restored leg back into dust and ran.

The spell obviously didn't work immediately, but he had no intention of finding out what it did. He was about to take advantage of the fact that no other mortal could see him.

He did a full sprint back to Black's Coffee and pushed through the door.

Black must have been having a really, really good time polishing cups because he was still doing it.

Claymore didn't care. He reached into Black's pocket and plucked out the keys for his truck—and Black didn't even notice.

Just when Claymore thought he was in the clear, he heard Lamia's rasping voice: "You really do take me for a fool, don't you?"

She was right behind him . . . but how was that possible? He'd gauged her regeneration time at around one or two minutes. There was no way she should have been able to follow him so quickly.

He didn't have time to react. As soon as he turned, she clamped her lizard claws around his neck and his gun clattered to the floor.

"I have walked this world for thousands of years!" she hissed, her deep green eyes staring into him. "You are a mortal! Blind! I was like you, once. I thought I was above the gods. I was the daughter of Hecate, goddess of magic. Zeus himself fell in love with me! I considered myself his equal! But then what did the gods do to me?"

Her hand closed tighter around his throat, and Claymore gasped for air. *"Hera slaughtered my children right in front of my eyes! She . . . ! That woman . . . !"*

A tear fell down her scaly face, but Claymore didn't care in the slightest about this creature's sob story. He drove his knee into her chest with as much force as he could muster and heard the satisfying crack of her ribs breaking.

Lamia fell backward. Hopefully, her ribs would take time to regenerate. She hunched over, wheezing, as if it were too painful for her to stand.

"I have already invoked the Temple of Fire," she said. "It is an incantation that destroys your sanctuary—whatever you most place your faith in. I may not be able to make you feel my pain, but I can still take away all that is precious to you! I can take away all of it in the wave of a hand!"

Suddenly the temperature in the café spiked. It felt like a sauna in which the heat kept building.

The tables were the first thing to catch, then the chairs, and then . . .

Claymore made a mad dash for Black, who was still happily polishing coffee cups.

"Incantare: Stulti Carcer!" Lamia shrieked.

Suddenly Claymore's legs felt like lead. He tried to force himself to move, but he couldn't. He was glued in place.

Flames began to creep up Black's apron. Soon his entire body was lit on fire. The worst part was that he didn't even notice what was happening to him.

Claymore cried out to him, but it was no use. He had to watch as his only real friend in Keeseville was consumed by flames in front of his eyes.

"Gods can do this!" Lamia cried. "They can erase everything that you hold dear in a second, and so shall I!" She turned to his laptop. "I'll destroy that, too—your latest work!"

She gestured at his computer as the flames rolled toward it across the bar. The plastic cover began melting. "Just try to save it, Claymore!" she taunted. "If you go and beat out the flames now, it might not be too late."

She flexed her hand and Claymore could suddenly feel his feet.

"Go, child of man," she hissed. "Save what is most precious to you. You will fail! Just like I—"

Lamia didn't have time to finish before Claymore's fist slammed into her face.

She crashed against a table. Claymore came down at her with another punch, his hand now coated with black sand. "How can you just stand there and talk like that after you've taken a man's life?" he cried.

She reached up at him with her clawed hands, but Claymore slapped them away. He overturned the table and she toppled to the floor.

"You killed him!" he shouted. "Burly had nothing to do with any of this, and you killed him! I don't care what kind of monster you are! By the time I'm done with you you're going to wish that *Hera* had killed you!"

She opened her mouth. *"Incantare: Stu—!"*

Claymore kicked her in the jaw, and the lower half of her face dissolved into sand.

The flames were getting harsher now. The acrid smoke burned in Claymore's lungs, but he didn't care. He kicked and punched Lamia into a pile of sand as she tried to regenerate, again and again.

Still . . . he knew he couldn't keep this up. He couldn't let his rage be the end of him. That's what Lamia wanted. She'd be fine regardless of anything he did to her, but he wasn't invulnerable— the smoke alone was making it hard to breathe. He had to get out of here. Otherwise, the pile of sand underneath his feet would have the last laugh.

It would take at least one minute for her to re-form, he guessed, just enough time for him to disappear.

He looked down at the swirling mass of powder, wondering if it could hear him. "By the time I see you next, I'll know how to kill you. Your death is inevitable. Once you grow legs again, I suggest you run."

He picked up his gun from the floor and fired into the pile of sand—one last shot for Burly Black.

It still wasn't enough. Justice had to be served, and if his hunch was right, he knew exactly the person to do it.

——— · ———

When the police discovered that he'd taken Black's truck, would they blame him for the fire? Would they accuse him of Black's murder?

A real monster was after him, but Claymore might be pegged as an enemy of the law. If the situation were different he would have found such irony funny; but not now, not when Black was dead.

Surely Black would have approved of Claymore taking his truck. . . . Claymore floored it, driving as fast as he possibly could without getting in an accident.

Lamia had an array of spells at her disposal. All Claymore had was a one-minute head start.

He didn't like those odds, but Claymore had a way of turning bad odds in his favor. He'd had no advantages in his life, yet he'd managed to get a PhD and become a successful author. Through his brilliance he'd made a name for himself. Even if he had been plunged into some strange world where monsters and gods existed, there was no way he'd allow himself to lose. Not to Lamia, not to Hecate, not to anyone.

He pulled into his driveway and ran inside, arming the alarm as he locked the door behind him.

He didn't plan to be here for more than a minute, but the alarm would give him some advance warning in case Lamia got here faster than he anticipated.

He tried to collect his thoughts. The boy Alabaster must have known about Lamia. In Claymore's dream, Alabaster had told the woman in white that he was being hunted. The woman had warned Alabaster that she couldn't interfere in a contest between her children. Which meant the woman in white was Hecate, and Lamia and Alabaster were both her children, locked in some sort of deadly struggle.

What happens if someone finds a way to stop death? the boy had asked him outside the auditorium. Alabaster needed a way to defeat Lamia, who couldn't die. Otherwise Lamia would kill *him*. So he'd turned to the foremost expert on death—Dr. Howard Claymore.

He picked up the card from his work desk and dialed the number into his cell phone. But the answer he got wasn't exactly a cry for help.

"What do you want?" the boy asked in a stone-cold tone. "I

know your answer was No. So what now? Do you want me to tell you that your dream last night wasn't real?"

"I'm not stupid," Claymore retorted, resetting the alarm on his way out. "I now know it was real, and I also know that your *sister* is trying to kill me. I was attacked in the shopping district, most likely because you asked me for help."

The boy seemed too stunned to speak. Finally, as Claymore was getting into Black's truck, Alabaster asked, "If she attacked you, how are you still alive?"

"As I said, I'm not an idiot," Claymore said. "But as a result of your dragging me into this, my friend is dead."

He explained briefly what had happened at Black's Coffee.

There was another moment of silence.

Claymore started the truck. "Well?"

"We need to stop talking," Alabaster said. "Monsters can track phone calls. Just come to my location and I'll explain what I need you to do. Hurry."

Claymore tossed his phone on the seat and slammed his foot down on the accelerator.

Alabaster's street was a cul-de-sac, a dead end with nothing behind it but limestone cliffs that dropped into the Hudson River. That meant there was no way they'd be attacked from behind, but it also meant that there was no running away.

It wasn't by chance that Alabaster had set up house here, Claymore assumed. Alabaster meant this to be a place where he could easily defend himself, even if he lost the option to retreat. A perfect place for a last stand.

In fact, number 273 was at the very end of the cul-de-sac.

It was nothing fancy, nothing special. The grass needed mowing and the walls needed a new coat of paint. It wasn't the nicest house in the world, but it was good enough for an average family to call home.

Claymore walked up to the door and knocked. It didn't take long for the door to open.

It was that man from yesterday, Alabaster's father. His blank eyes scanned Claymore, and he smiled. "Hello, friend! Come on in. I've made tea for you."

Claymore frowned. "I honestly don't care at this point. Just bring me to your son."

Still smiling, the man ushered Claymore inside.

Unlike the outside, the living room was meticulous. Everything was perfectly polished, straightened, and dusted. It looked like all the furniture had just come out of plastic wrap.

A fire roared in the fireplace, and as promised, tea was sitting on the coffee table.

Claymore ignored it. He sat down on the sofa. "Mr. Torrington, correct? You *do* understand the situation I'm in? I came here for answers."

"The tea's going to get cold," the man reported, smiling cheerfully. "Drink up!"

Claymore looked him in the eyes. *This* was his secret weapon? "Are you stupid?"

The man didn't get to respond before a door opened to the main room, and the boy walked in.

Same freckles and brown hair as yesterday, but his outfit was downright bizarre. He wore a bulletproof vest over a long-sleeved, dark gray shirt. His pants were gray as well, but the oddest thing about his clothes was the symbols.

Nonsensical markings were scribbled in random places all over his shirt and trousers. It looked like he'd let some five-year-old go crazy with a green Sharpie.

"Dr. Claymore," he said, "don't bother talking to my companion. He won't tell you anything interesting."

All of the nervousness and anxiety seemed to be gone from the boy. He stood grim and determined, like the moment he had tried to mock Claymore in the auditorium.

Claymore glanced at the man, then back at Alabaster. "Why not? Isn't he your father?"

Alabaster laughed. "No." He plopped down on the sofa and grabbed a cup of tea. "He's a Mistform. I created him to serve as my guardian so people don't ask questions."

Claymore's eyes widened. He looked at the man, who seemed completely oblivious to their conversation. "Created? With magic, you mean?"

Alabaster nodded, reaching into his pocket and pulling out a blank note card. He placed it on the table and tapped it twice.

The man, the Mistform, disintegrated right in front of Claymore's eyes, melting into vapor as he was sucked into the card. Once the Mistform was gone, Alabaster picked up the card, and Claymore could see that there was now a crude green outline of a man imprinted on it.

"There, that's better." Alabaster managed a smile. "He gets annoying after a while. I know this must be a lot to take in for a mortal."

"I'll manage," Claymore said, dismissing him. "I'm more interested in learning about Lamia, particularly a way to kill her."

Alabaster sighed. "I told you already, I don't know. That's why I asked for your help. Do you remember what I asked you in the parking lot?"

"What would happen if someone found a way to stop death?" Claymore repeated. "Why is that important? Does it have something to do with Lamia's regeneration?"

"No, all monsters do that. There are only two ways to kill a monster: One is with some sort of godly metal. The other is with some form of binding magic that stops them from re-forming in this world. But killing her isn't the problem; I've done that. The problem is that she won't die."

Claymore raised an eyebrow. "What do you mean, *won't die*?"

"Exactly what it sounds like," Alabaster said. "If I kill her, she doesn't stay dead, no matter what I try. When most monsters disintegrate, their spirits go back to Tartarus and it takes years, maybe centuries before they can regenerate. But Lamia comes back immediately. That's why I came to you. I know you've researched the spiritual aspects of death, probably more than anyone else in this world. I was hoping that you could figure out a way to keep something dead."

Claymore thought about it for a second, then shook his head. "I want nothing more than to destroy that creature, but this is beyond me. I need to understand your world better—how these gods and monsters operate, and the rules of your magic. I need data."

Alabaster frowned and took a sip of tea. "I'll tell you what I can, but we may not have much time. Lamia is getting better and better at seeing through my concealment spells."

Claymore leaned back. "In my dream, Hecate said that you were a member of the army of Kronos. Surely there are other members of your army. Why not ask them for help?"

Alabaster shook his head. "Most of them are dead. There was a war between the gods and Titans last summer and most half-bloods—demigods like me—fought for the Olympians. I fought for Kronos."

The boy took a shaky breath before continuing. "Our main transport ship, the *Princess Andromeda*, was obliterated by an enemy faction of half-bloods. We were sailing to invade Manhattan, where the gods have their base. I was on our ship when the enemy half-bloods blew it up. I only survived because I was able to put an incantation of protection on myself. After that, well . . . the war didn't go our way. I fought on the battlefield against the enemy, but most of our allies ran. Kronos himself marched on Olympus, only to be killed by a son of Poseidon. After Kronos's death, the Olympian gods smashed any remaining resistance. It was a massacre. If I remember right, my mother told me that Camp Half-Blood and its allies had sixteen casualties total. We had hundreds."

Claymore eyed Alabaster. Though Claymore wouldn't call himself empathetic, he did feel sorry for this boy, having gone through so much at such a young age. "If your forces were completely destroyed, how did you escape?"

"We weren't all destroyed," Alabaster said. "Most of the remaining half-bloods fled or were captured. They were so demoralized they joined the enemy. There was a general amnesty, I guess you'd call it—a deal negotiated by the same kid who killed Kronos. That kid convinced the Olympians to accept the *minor* gods who'd followed Kronos."

"Like your mother, Hecate," Claymore said.

"Yes," Alabaster said bitterly. "Camp Half-Blood decided that they would accept any children of minor gods. They would build us cabins at camp and pretend that they didn't just blindly massacre us for resisting. Most of the minor gods accepted the peace deal as soon as the Olympians proposed it, but my mother didn't. You see . . . I wasn't the only child of Hecate serving under Kronos. Hecate never had many children—but I was the strongest, so my siblings followed my lead. I convinced most of them to fight . . . but I was the only one who survived. Hecate lost more demigod children in that war than any other god."

"That's why she refused their offer?" Claymore guessed.

Alabaster took another sip of tea. "Yes. At least, she refused it at first. I urged her to keep fighting. But the gods decided that they didn't want one rebellious goddess to spoil their victory, so they made her a deal. They would exile me forever from their favor and their camp—that was my punishment for having an attitude—but they would spare my life if Hecate rejoined them. Which is another way of saying that if she *didn't* join them, they'd make sure I died."

Claymore frowned. "So even the gods aren't high and almighty enough to resist blackmail."

Alabaster stared at the cozy fireplace with a look of distaste. "It's better not to imagine them as gods. The best way to think of them is more like a divine Mafia. They used their threat to force my mother into accepting the deal. And in the process, exile me from camp so I can't *corrupt* my brothers and sisters." He finished his tea. "But I'll never bow to the Olympian gods after the atrocities they committed. Their followers are blind. I'd never set foot in their camp, and if I did, it would only be to give that son of Poseidon what he deserves."

"So you have no help," Claymore said. "And this monster Lamia is after you . . . why?"

"I wish I knew." Alabaster put down his empty cup. "Since the moment I was exiled, I've fought and killed a lot of monsters that came after me. They instinctively sense demigods. As a lone half-blood, I'm a tempting target. But Lamia is different. She's a child of Hecate from the ancient days. She seems to have a personal vendetta against me. No matter how many times I kill her, she just won't stay dead. She's been wearing me down, forcing me to move from town to town. My protective incantations have been pushed to their breaking point. Now I can't even sleep without her trying to break through my barriers."

Claymore studied the boy more closely and noticed dark circles under his eyes. Alabaster probably hadn't slept in days.

"How long ago have you been on your own?" Claymore asked. "When was your banishment?"

Alabaster shrugged like even he'd forgotten. "Seven or eight months ago, but it seems longer. Time is different for us half-bloods. We don't have the same cushy lives that mortals do. Most half-bloods don't even live past twenty."

Claymore didn't reply. Even for him, this was a lot to absorb. This child was an actual demigod, the son of a human and the goddess Hecate.

He had no idea how that sort of procreation worked, but obviously it did, because the boy was here, and clearly he was no regular mortal. Claymore wondered if Alabaster shared Lamia's ability of regeneration. He doubted it. Siblings or not, Alabaster constantly referred to Lamia as a monster. That wasn't the kind of term you'd use for your own kind.

The boy was truly alone. The gods had exiled him. Monsters wanted to kill him, including one who was his own sister. His only companion was a Mistborn man who sprang from a three-by-five note card. And yet somehow, the child had survived. Claymore couldn't help being impressed.

Alabaster started to pour himself another cup of tea, then froze. One of the symbols scribbled onto his right sleeve was glowing bright green.

"Lamia's here," he muttered. "I have enough power to keep her out for a while, but—"

There was a brittle sound like a lightbulb popping, and the symbol on his sleeve splintered like glass, spraying shards of green light.

Alabaster dropped his cup. "That's impossible! There's no way she could have broken my barrier with her magic unless she . . ." He stared at Claymore. "My gods. Claymore, she's using you!"

Claymore tensed. "Using me? What are you talking about?"

Before Alabaster could answer, another rune on his shirt exploded. "Get up! We need to go now! She just breached the secondary barrier."

Claymore got to his feet. "Wait! Tell me! How is she using me?"

"You didn't escape her; she let you go!" Alabaster glared at him. "You have an incantation on you that disrupted my spell insignias! Gods, how could I have been so stupid!"

Claymore clenched his fists. He'd been outplayed.

He'd been so busy trying to comprehend the rules of this world and form a strategy that he hadn't expected Lamia to use a strategy of her own. Now his mistakes had led her right to her target.

Alabaster touched Claymore lightly on the chest. *"Incantare: Aufero Sarcina!"*

There was another explosion. This time green shards of light flew from Claymore's shirt and he staggered backward. "What did you—?"

"Removing Lamia's incantation," Alabaster explained. "And now . . ."

Alabaster tapped a few more runes on his outfit and they all shattered. As if in response, a symbol on his pants leg started to glow bright green.

"I've strengthened the inner walls, but there's no way they'll hold her long. I know you want to understand, I know you want to ask more questions, but don't. I'm not going to let you die. Just follow me, and hurry!"

———————

So far today, he'd been confused, alarmed, afraid, and aggravated beyond belief. But now he experienced an emotion he hadn't felt in years. The great, confident Dr. Claymore started to panic.

All of it was a trap. Lamia wasn't defeated so easily. It was a trick so that she could get through Alabaster's defenses. And all of it was his fault.

Alabaster ran outside, and Claymore followed, muttering every curse he knew—and there were quite a few.

He hadn't seen it before, but a flickering green dome covered the entire house and stretched down at least half of the block. The green glow seemed to be weakening, and so was the rune on Alabaster's leg.

Even though it had been bright and sunny just moments ago, storm clouds now hovered overhead, bombarding the barrier with lightning strikes.

Lamia was out there, and this time she wasn't playing games. She was here to kill them.

Claymore muttered another curse.

Alabaster stopped when he got to the street and looked up at the sky. "We can't escape. She's locked us in. This storm is a binding incantation. I can't dispel it while the barrier's up. Running isn't an option; we have to fight."

Claymore stared at him in disbelief. "Black's truck is right there. We can take the truck and—"

"And then what?" Alabaster stared back, freezing Claymore in place. "It doesn't matter how fast we drive. All we're doing is giving her is a bigger target to hit. Besides, that's exactly what she'd expect a mortal like you to do. Just stay out of this—I'm trying to save your life!"

Claymore glared at him, his blood boiling. He'd come here to help this boy, not stand around feeling useless. He was about to argue when the glowing rune on Alabaster's leg burst into flame. The boy winced in pain, falling to his knees. Above them, the green dome shattered with a sound like a million windows breaking.

"Brother!" Lamia cried over the roar of thunder. "I'm here!"

Lightning struck all around them, taking out electrical poles and setting trees ablaze.

The rest of the world didn't even seem to notice. A few houses away, a man was watering his lawn. Across the street, a woman trotted out to her SUV, chatting on her cell phone, oblivious to the fact that her maple tree was on fire. The same kind of flames that had killed Burly . . . Apparently to half-bloods and monsters, the mortal world was just collateral damage.

Alabaster forced himself up, pulling a flash card from his pocket. Instead of a man, this card had the inscription of a crudely drawn sword on it. When Alabaster tapped the drawing it started to glow, and suddenly the sword wasn't so crude.

A solid gold broadsword extended from the card, glistening into reality and forming in Alabaster's hand. The sword was etched with glowing green runes, like the ones on Alabaster's clothes. And even though the thing must have weighed a hundred pounds, Alabaster held it in one hand with ease.

"Get behind me and don't move," he said, planting his feet firmly on the ground.

For once in his life, Claymore didn't even try to argue.

"Lamia!" Alabaster shouted at the sky. "Former queen of the Libyan empire and daughter of Hecate! You are my target, and my blade finds you. *Incantare: Persequor Vestigium!*"

The symbols on Alabaster's sword blazed even more fiercely, and every single rune on his clothes shone like miniature spot-lights. A collage of magical spells surrounded him, and his entire body seemed to radiate power.

He turned to Claymore, who took a step back. Both of Alabaster's eyes were flashing green, just like Lamia's.

The boy smiled. "We'll be fine, Claymore. Heroes never die, right?"

Claymore wanted to argue that, in fact, the heroes *always* seemed to die in Greek myths.

But before he could find his voice, thunder roared, and the monster Lamia appeared at the edge of the lawn.

Alabaster charged.

———

As Alabaster raised his sword, he felt something he hadn't felt since he'd invaded Manhattan with Kronos's army—the willingness to give his life in the name of a cause. He'd dragged Claymore into this. He could not let another mortal die because of this monster.

His first swing was a hit, and Lamia's right arm disintegrated into sand.

To normal monsters, a wound like that from an Imperial gold sword would be a death sentence, but all Lamia did was laugh.

"Brother, why do you persist? I only came here to talk. . . ."

"Lies!" Alabaster spat, lopping off her left arm. "You're a disgrace to our mother's name! Why don't you die?"

Lamia gave him a smile of crocodile teeth. "I don't die because my mistress sustains me."

"Your mistress?" Alabaster scowled. He had a feeling she wasn't talking about Hecate.

"Oh, yes." Lamia dodged his strike. Her arms were already

re-forming. "Kronos failed, but now my mistress has risen. She is greater than any Titan or god. She will destroy Olympus and lead the children of Hecate to their golden age. Unfortunately, my mistress doesn't trust you. She doesn't want you alive to interfere."

"You and your mistress can go to Tartarus for all I care!" Alabaster roared, slicing Lamia's head clean down the middle. "Are you in league with the gods now? Did Hera send you to kill me?"

The two halves of Lamia's mouth wailed. "Do *not* mention that name in my presence! That crone destroyed my family! Don't you understand, brother? Haven't you read my myths?"

Alabaster sneered. "I don't bother reading about worthless monsters like you!"

"Monster?" she shrieked as her face mended. *"Hera* is the monster! She destroys all the women her husband falls in love with. She hunts down their offspring out of jealousy and spite! She killed my children! *My children!"*

Lamia's right arm re-formed, and she held it in front of her, trembling with rage. "I can still see their lifeless bodies in front of me. . . . Altheia wanted to be an artist. I remember the days when she apprenticed under my kingdom's finest sculptors. . . . She was a child protégé. Her skills rivaled even those of Athena. Demetrius was nine, five days from his tenth birthday. He was a wonderful and strong boy, always trying to make his mother proud. He was willing to do anything in order to prepare for the day he took his place as king of Libya. They both worked so hard, they both had amazing futures ahead of them. But then what did Hera do? She brutally murdered them simply to punish me for accepting Zeus's courtship! She's the one who deserves to rot in Tartarus!"

Alabaster swung again. This time Lamia did the impossible— she stopped the blade, catching the Imperial gold edge with her reptilian claw.

Alabaster tried to pull his sword free, but Lamia held it fast. She put her face close to his.

"You know what happened next, brother?" she whispered. Her breath smelled like freshly spilled blood. "My life as queen may have been over, but my hatred was just beginning. Using Mother's power I crafted a very special incantation, one that allowed all the monsters in the world to sense the taint of half-bloods . . ." She smiled. "Maybe after a few thousand more of you die, Hera, the goddess of family, will finally understand my pain!"

Alabaster caught his breath. "What did you just say?"

"Yes, you heard me! I was the one who made all of your lives a living nightmare! I gave monsters the ability to track demigods! I am the Lamia, the butcher of the tainted! And once you are dead, our other siblings will follow me as their queen. They will join me or die! My mistress—Mother Earth herself—has promised she will return my children to me." Lamia laughed with delight. "They will live again, and all I have to do is kill you!"

Alabaster managed to tug his sword from her grip, but Lamia was too close. She thrust out her claws to tear out his heart. There was a sharp *BANG!* and Lamia staggered backward, a bullet hole in her scaly chest. Alabaster swung his blade, cutting her in half at the waist, and Lamia crumbled into a pile of black sand.

Alabaster glanced back at Claymore, who was standing ten feet to his right, holding a gun. "What are you doing here? She could have killed you!"

Claymore smiled. "I saw that you were doing just as pitiful a job as I, so I thought I'd lend a hand. I had to do something with my last bullet."

Alabaster stared at him in amazement. "Gods, you really are arrogant."

"I've heard that a lot lately. I'm going to start taking it as a compliment." Claymore looked down at Lamia's body, which was already re-forming. "A Swiffer would be helpful right now. She'll be back any minute."

Alabaster tried to think, but he felt exhausted. Most of his incantations were gone. His defenses were destroyed. "We have to get out of here."

Claymore shook his head. "Running hasn't helped you before. We need a way to deal with her. She said her life was sustained by her mistress . . ."

"Mother Earth," Alabaster said. "Gaea. She tried to overthrow the gods once before in the ancient times. But how does that help us?"

Claymore picked up a handful of black sand and watched it writhing, trying to re-form. "Earth . . ." he mused. "If sending Lamia back to Tartarus doesn't work, if she won't stay dead, isn't there a way to imprison her on *this* earth?"

Alabaster frowned. Then a lightbulb went off in his head.

He had expected this man, this genius, to have a more complicated answer. Alabaster expected that if he told Claymore about the Underworld and what caused death for monsters, the best mind of the century could tell him how to kill Lamia permanently.

But the answer was much simpler than that. Claymore had just unwittingly solved the problem.

They couldn't *kill* Lamia for good. The earth goddess Gaea would simply let her back into the mortal world again and again. But what if they didn't *try* to send her to Tartarus? What if *this* earth became Lamia's prison instead?

Alabaster looked him in the eyes. "We have to get back inside my house! I think I know a way to stop her."

"Are you sure?" Claymore asked. "How?"

Alabaster shook his head. "No time! Just look for the book on my nightstand. If we get that, we can stop her. Now go!"

Claymore nodded, and they ran toward the front door.

Alabaster had had the power to stop her all along and he just hadn't known it. But now he had the answer. And there wasn't a monster in the world that could stop him.

———————

Claymore was tired of running.

His young friend Alabaster looked like he could still go for miles despite the hundred-pound sword he was carrying. And Alabaster had been withstanding Lamia's attacks for weeks.

Claymore was a different story. After evading Lamia for only a few hours, he was about to collapse. Half-bloods must have been made of sterner stuff than humans.

Alabaster tore through the living room. He glanced back, grinning ear-to-ear, and gestured at Claymore to hurry. "It was here all along! Gods, I wish I had known!"

Thunder cracked outside, and Claymore frowned. "You can save that talk for after we win. Let's hope your magic bullet actually works."

Alabaster nodded. "I'm sure of it! Every form of invincibility has a weak point. Tanks have a hatch, Achilles had a heel, and Lamia has this."

Looking at Alabaster's expression, Claymore almost smiled. *This* was the happy-go-lucky boy that he was supposed to be—not a half-blood warrior who expected to die by the age of twenty.

He seemed like a normal sixteen-year-old with a full life ahead of him. . . .

Maybe after Lamia was dead, Alabaster could live that life. Maybe, if the gods would let him have it. . . .

But what was *Claymore* going to do? His entire life had been devoted to finding an answer to death, but in the past day he'd discovered that everything he'd come to believe was a lie. Or rather, the lies he'd dismissed all his life were actually true.

How was Claymore supposed to make a difference now? How could a middle-aged man with no special powers even start to affect a world of gods and monsters?

His old life seemed meaningless—his deadlines, his book signings. That life had melted along with his laptop in Black's Coffee. Would this new world even have a place for a mortal like him?

Alabaster led him up the stairs and into a small bedroom. The walls were covered in the same green runes that were on Alabaster's clothing. All of them glowed to life as he walked inside and picked up the notebook from his nightstand.

"This is a shorthand incantation," he explained. "I'm sure it will work. It has to!"

The boy turned toward Claymore, who was waiting at the door. Alabaster's smile melted. His expression changed to horror.

A split second later Claymore realized why. Cold claws pricked against the back of his neck. Lamia's voice crackled next to his ear.

"If you speak one word of that incantation, I'll kill him," Lamia threatened. "Drop the book, and perhaps I'll spare his life."

Claymore stared at the boy, expecting him to read the spell anyway, but like an idiot, he dropped the book.

"What are you doing?" Claymore growled. "Read the spell!"

Alabaster was frozen, like a thousand people were looking at him. "I—I can't. . . . She'll—"

"Don't think about me!" Claymore yelled, as Lamia dug her claws deeper into his neck.

Then she whispered by his ear: *"Incantare: Templum Incendere."*

The book at Alabaster's feet burst into flame.

"What are you doing, you idiot?" Claymore roared at the boy. "You're smarter than that, Alabaster! If you don't read that spell, you will die too!"

A tear traced its way down Alabaster's cheek. "Don't you understand? I don't want anyone else to die because of me. I led my siblings to their deaths!"

Claymore scowled. Could the boy not *see* the book burning?

Lamia cackled as the notebook's cover curled to ashes. The pages wouldn't last much longer. There was no time to convince the thickheaded boy. Claymore would have to spur him into action.

"Alabaster . . . what happens when we die?"

"Stop saying that!" Alabaster screamed. "You're going to be fine!"

But Claymore just shook his head. He was the only thing keeping Alabaster from reading the book, so the path he had to take was clear. He had to destroy the last obstacle in Alabaster's way.

To avenge Burly, to save this one child from the gods, he knew what he had to do.

"Alabaster, you told me earlier that heroes don't die. You may be right, but I can tell you one thing." Claymore looked the boy in the eyes. "I'm not a hero."

With that Claymore pushed back against Lamia. They both tumbled into the hall. Claymore turned and tried to grapple with the monster, hoping to buy Alabaster a few seconds, but he knew he couldn't win this fight.

Alabaster's horrified scream reached him from far away. Then he was drifting, drifting into another world. Death's cold hand wrapped around Howard Claymore like an icy prison.

———·———

There was no ferryman for him, not even a boat. He was dragged through the bone-chilling water of the Styx, pulled toward whatever punishment awaited him for the life that he had led.

He could try to claim he was a man of pure motives, trying to preach sense to the world, but even he knew that wasn't the truth. He had dismissed the mere idea of gods and been dismissive of anyone who worshipped one. They all had been just a laugh to him—but if he'd learned anything from the last six hours, it was that these gods didn't have a sense of humor.

Pity was, he thought to himself as he was pulled through the icy current, if Alabaster wasn't an enemy of the gods, Claymore might have been received as a hero for saving the boy's life.

But fate had a different plan for him. When he was facing his judgment, he would also have to be punished for aiding a traitor.

It was ironic, really. . . . He had died doing a good thing, but he might be sentenced to an eternity in darkness. This had been his fear from childhood, dying and being rejected by heaven.

Of course, even as he floated through the frigid waters, he had a smile on his face.

The fact that Alabaster wasn't making this journey with him told him one thing: Lamia hadn't killed the boy. Without a hostage holding him back, surely Alabaster would have read the spell out of pure rage and defeated Lamia.

And that was enough to make Claymore content, no matter what punishment the gods decided on.

He'd have the last laugh now, and for the rest of eternity.

But, surprisingly, fate didn't play out that way. Above him in the darkness, a light glimmered, growing brighter and warmer. A hand reached down to him—a woman's hand reached out to him through the darkness. Being a logical man, he did the logical thing. He took it.

Once his eyes adjusted, he saw that he was in a church. Not the glistening holy church of heaven, but one that had fallen into disrepair. It was the same filthy, dust-covered chapel that he had seen in his dreams. And praying at the altar was the young woman in ceremonial clothing—Alabaster's mom, the goddess Hecate.

"I suppose you're waiting for me to thank you," Claymore said. "For saving my life, that is."

"No," Hecate said, solemnly. "Because I didn't save your life. You're still dead."

Claymore's first instinct was to argue, but he didn't. It doesn't take a genius to figure out your heart isn't beating. "Then why am I here? Why did you bring me to this place?"

He approached the altar and sat in the dust next to Hecate, but she didn't look at him. She kept her eyes closed and prayed. Her face was like a Greek statue—pale, beautiful, and ageless.

"I saved *them*," she told him. "Both of my children. You're going to hate me for that."

Both . . . She'd saved Lamia. . . .

Claymore guessed it wasn't wise to yell at a goddess, but he couldn't help it. "You told Alabaster you couldn't interfere!" he demanded. "After all I sacrificed to help the boy, you stepped in at the last moment and saved that monster?"

"I don't want any more of my children to die," Hecate said.

"Alabaster's solution would have worked. Thanks to your selfless death, he had time to retrieve the notebook and find the spell. It was a binding incantation—the reversal of a spell designed to heal and fortify a living body. If he had cast it on Lamia she would have been reduced to a pile of black dust, but she would not have died. Nor would she have regenerated. She would have remained alive as a pile of black dust forever. I stopped that before it could happen."

Claymore blinked. The boy's solution would have been both brilliant and simple. He admired Alabaster more than ever.

"Why didn't you let him do it?" Claymore asked. "Lamia is a murderer. Didn't she deserve Alabaster's judgment?"

Hecate didn't answer for a moment. She just clasped her hands tighter.

After what seemed like an eternity of silence, she whispered: "Alabaster likes you. I saw how happy you make him. It's probably because you remind us both of his father." She smiled faintly. "Alabaster is a child who always seeks to make his mother proud, even if he can sometimes be reckless. . . . But Lamia also had a difficult past. She didn't ask for her fate. I want to see her as happy as Alabaster."

"Did you bring me here just to tell me this?" Claymore asked, raising an eyebrow. "To tell me that all of my efforts were in vain?"

"They won't be, Doctor. Because I'm going to have you look after Alabaster."

He eyed her curiously. "And how do I do that if I'm dead?"

"My main role as a goddess is maintaining the Mist, the magical barrier between the Olympian and mortal worlds. I keep those two worlds apart. When mortals do get a glimpse of something magical, I come up with happy alternatives for them to believe in. Alabaster also has power over the Mist. I'm sure he showed you some of his creations—symbols that can been turned into solid objects."

"Mistforms." Claymore recalled the fake father and the golden sword. "Yes, Alabaster gave me a demonstration."

Hecate's expression turned more serious. "Recently the boundaries between life and death have been weakened, thanks to the goddess Gaea. This is how she can bring her monstrous servants back from the underworld so quickly, make them regenerate almost immediately. But I can use this weakness to our advantage. I could return your soul to the world in a Mistform body. It would take much of my own power, but I could give you a new life. Alabaster has always been headstrong and impatient, but if you're by his side, you can guide him."

Claymore stared at the goddess. Returning to life as a Mistform . . . he had to admit it sounded better than eternal punishment. "If you have so much power, why couldn't you separate Lamia and Alabaster earlier? Wasn't my death unnecessary?"

"Unfortunately, Doctor, your death was very necessary," Hecate said. "Magic cannot create something from nothing. It makes use of what already exists. A noble sacrifice creates powerful magic energy. I *used* that force to separate my children. In effect, your death allowed me to save them both. Perhaps more important, Alabaster learned something from your death. And I suspect you did, too."

Claymore bit back a retort. He didn't appreciate his death being used as a lesson.

"What if it just happens again?" Claymore asked. "Won't Lamia continue to go after your son?"

"In the short term, no," Hecate said. "Alabaster now has a powerful spell to defeat her. She would be foolish to attack."

"But eventually she'll find a way to counter that spell," Claymore guessed.

Hecate sighed. "It may come to that. My children have always fought with one another. The strongest leads the others. Alabaster joined Kronos's cause and led his siblings to war. He blames himself for their deaths. Now Lamia has risen up to challenge his preeminence, hoping the children of magic will follow her under Gaea's banner. There must be another way. The other gods have never trusted my offspring, but this Gaean rebellion will only bring more bloodshed. Alabaster must find another answer—some new arrangement that will bring peace to my children."

Claymore hesitated. "And if they don't *want* peace?"

"I will not choose sides," she said, "but I hope with you there to guide him, Alabaster will make the right decision, a decision that will lead my family to peace."

A reason to live, Claymore thought. A way for one mortal man with no special powers to affect the world of gods and monsters.

Claymore smiled. "That sounds like a challenge. Very well, I accept. And though I will be only a Mistform, I'll make sure he succeeds."

He stood, about to walk out the doors of the church, but then he stopped.

Even if he was dead, the answer he was seeking was right in front of him.

"I have one more question to ask you, Hecate." He steeled his tongue, just as Alabaster must have done in front of the audience at his lecture. "If you yourself are a deity, who are you praying to?"

She paused for a moment, turned to him, and opened her brilliant green eyes. Then, as though the answer were obvious, she smiled and said, "I hope you find out."

———

Alabaster woke up in a field. All of the runes on his clothing had been shattered, and his bulletproof vest was slashed past the point of being usable.

Surprisingly, though, he felt fine.

He lay there in the grass for a minute, trying to figure out where he was. His last memories were of Claymore slamming into the monster, Lamia's claws closing on the doctor's neck, the burning notebook, the incantation . . . He'd been ready to cast the spell, and then . . . he'd woken up here.

He reached into his pocket and pulled out his Mistform cards; but all the inscriptions had turned to black smudges—spent, along with the rest of his magic.

Then a man's shape appeared over him, blocking the sunlight. A hand reached down to help him up.

"Claymore?" Alabaster's spirits lifted immediately. "What happened? I thought . . . What are you *doing* here?"

Claymore gave Alabaster a smile that would last him the rest of his life. "Come on," he said. "I think the two of us have some research to do."

RICK RIORDAN is the author of the *New York Times* #1 best-selling *The Son of Neptune* and *The Lost Hero*, the first two books in his Heroes of Olympus series. He also penned the *New York Times* #1 best-selling Percy Jackson and the Olympians series: Book One: *The Lightning Thief*; Book Two: *The Sea of Monsters*; Book Three: *The Titan's Curse*; Book Four: *The Battle of the Labyrinth*; and Book Five: *The Last Olympian*. The three books in his Kane Chronicles, based on Egyptian mythology, *The Red Pyramid*, *The Throne of Fire*, and *The Serpent's Shadow*, were *New York Times* best sellers as well. Rick lives in San Antonio, Texas, with his wife and two sons. To learn more about him, visit his website at www.rickriordan.com.